Firestorm.

Book one of the Maelstrom MC Series

Scarlett J Rose

Thank-You!

To my editor, Susan Horsnell, again, thank you for your hard work and effort in editing and being an awesome friend, and a woman of awesome talent!

To my friend, J… you know who you are! Thank you for your insight and leading me through the prickly bits that I got a little bit wrong!

To Cherry Shepard, you sexy thang, you! Thank you for letting me borrow the Devil's Rogues in the first chapter. (This is another talented lady, and one of the first Authors I read on my tablet when I got my kindle app, so I got mad love for this one!)

And to my readers, I hope you enjoy my first foray into the world of Maelstrom!

Mad, Mad Love.

-   Scarlett J Rose

January 2017.

Firestorm

Book one of the Maelstrom MC Series

Scarlett J Rose.

Chapter One

1989, Chicago, Illinois.

The engine growled like a beast waiting to be unleashed as it idled between his thighs. His heart beat in a steady and calm rhythm, the cold of the gun's muzzle against the skin of his lower back reassured him he could take on anything that life threw at him. Brett 'Firebird' Collins, a prospect for the Maelstrom MC, and son of their chapter's president watched and waited for the handover.

Tank, his best friend and fellow prospect sat beside him on his own Harley; it too growled out its desire to be running the lines of the open road. The two young men watched as their Sargent at Arms made the trade, cash for cocaine, with their contact from the Devil's Rogues MC.

The boys were running security with Dagger, and so far, things had gone very smoothly. Dagger nodded to the boys, who got off their bikes and helped to load up the blocks into their saddlebags. Their ride home would be uneventful, just the way his father, Dozer, the club's President, liked things to be. Quiet and under the radar.

The freedom the open road offered gave Firebird a sense of peace in their bloody world. At seventeen he had told his father that he wanted to join the club. His mother had been adamant to keep away from the club and the bloody history that it had. But the young man's stubbornness, and his father's guidance had steered him away from his mother's wishes for him to lead a 'normal life'.

The club voted Firebird and Tank in as prospects. His mother cried in her room for almost a week, afraid that she would lose her baby boy to the life.

Shortly after they'd been brought in as prospects, their rivals, the Sons of Abaddon MC, started a war with the Maelstrom over turf and drugs. Firebird had been cornered while working security for a bar and beaten. Tank's pet dog had been stolen from his yard. Tank had also been grabbed from his bed the same night. They held Tank down and forced him to watch as Johnny Pope, The Abaddon V.P. and some of his men used the dog in a fighting ring. The animal didn't survive the brutal fight.

They hauled the body of the animal from the ring and set it alight in a dumpster out the back, dragging Tank and holding his head up to force him to watch as the flames leapt and turned the broken body black. When the flames died down, Johnny turned to his men, with a nod, they beat Tank until he was barely conscious.

"Fucking weak, like all Maelstrom whelps."
Johnny had said after viciously kicking Tank in the
stomach and spitting on him before they left the bloodied
and beaten young man on the ground.

Firebird found his best friend beaten and
bloodied, cradling the still smoking remains of his poor
dog, sobbing inconsolably. Firebird had taken the
gasoline can that the bastards had used to douse Tank's
dog and returned the favour, setting the Sons of Abaddon
VP's prized 1974 Pontiac Firebird ablaze out the front of
the brothel where the V.P. was getting his weekly
blowjob from the woman who owned the place.

Johnny had run out to find his prized car ablaze,
his pants had dropped down around his ankles and he
had stood with his hands gripping his hair in a mixture of
despair and anger while exposing his lipstick-covered
dick to the world.

Firebird had then hightailed it to the safety of the
Maelstrom MC clubhouse, where they explained to
Firebird's father what had happened. He agreed with his
son's method of vengeance, commending him on his
dedication to the club.

That had been over a year ago, and so far, both
Tank and Firebird had proven themselves time and
again, earning the respect from their brothers in the MC.
Tank had changed from a sensitive young man to a

hardened one in that time. He had a way with dogs and hated to see any cruelty to animals. He'd personally rescued a few dogs that he had gone on to train as guard dogs for the MC's compound.

With their business concluded earlier that morning, the trio rode back to New York State, where their quiet little town was nestled just over the border with Pennsylvania. They made it back into the compound as night was falling, a long, hard ride behind them.

Firebird nodded to the figure watching from the second story window, the meeting room where Church was held and his father awaited.

"Boys." Their VP, Ollie, bellowed as he exited the door. "The Prez wants a word, get your sorry fuckin' asses in Church now!"

Firebird and Tank had barely enough time to set their kickstands down and scramble off their bikes before they were grabbed by a couple of the brothers and hauled up the stairs to the meeting room, where the rest of the patched brothers waited.

Firebird's father looked grim, making the young man think he'd done something wrong. He wracked his brains, working his gray matter trying to figure it out, but he came up empty.

"Son, if you haven't figured it out yet, then I don't know what to tell you." His father shook his head.

Firebird hated to disappoint his old man. He lowered his head, crestfallen, but confused as to what he could possibly have done wrong.

"Take your fucking cuts off, both of you and those top rockers off."

Firebird and Tank looked at each other. Firebird felt as if the world had dropped out from beneath him. And Tank, well, he looked like he had just lost the only family he had ever known, which in part was true. His mother had abandoned him and his father was a drunk, not worthy of the title 'father.' So, naturally the young man gravitated towards the MC for its values on brotherhood.

They pulled their cuts from their shoulders and laid them on the table, Firebird pulled his pocket knife out and sliced through the stitches that bound his bottom rocker taking care not to damage the thick black leather of his cut, before he handed the knife to Tank who followed suit. Firebird looked at his father, a deadpan look returned to the young man.

"So, you think you got what it takes to wear a Maelstrom rocker?" his father asked him.

Firebird looked at his old man, surprise evident on his face, he quickly let his mask return before he answered his father.

"Yeah, I do. I think Tank's got what it takes as well." He nodded to his brother in all but blood and name.

"Good, so do we. Put these on, Brothers." Firebird's father grinned as Sucker, their secretary tossed a couple of curved Maelstrom MC top rockers their way.

Tank laughed, as he caught his, and spread it out on the leather cut which had once held the words 'prospect' on a semicircular rocker. Firebird's father got to his feet and embraced his son and new brother.

"Welcome, brothers, to the Maelstrom MC, New York Chapter." He held his son close. "So proud of you, boy," He whispered against Firebird's ear.

"Thanks, Dad." Firebird grinned.

Tank and Firebird both endured the rough hugs the men gave them, slaps on their backs and the occasional good-natured punch to the arm.

***

The real party began as soon as they settled back downstairs, where the club whores, the Storm Girls were waiting to bring them to their knees with the pleasures of their flesh and copious amounts of alcohol.

Firebird grinned at Tank, who had a beer in one hand and a club whore's head in his lap.

"Fuck Brother, does it get any better than this?" he asked as the blonde's head bobbed up and down, the suckling noises from her mouth made Firebird's cock stand to attention.

"Nope, I don't think so, brother." Firebird grinned as he raised a beer in toast to his brother.

Chapter Two

"I don't fucking believe this!" Jenna said, shaking her head. She looked over the roster again, Vladimir had her working another afternoon shift which would conflict with her classes *again*.

She stormed through the empty seating area of the strip club. On stage, Rosie and Jackie worked the poles to the Tuesday 'crowd' - die hard regulars while Joey and Viktor, who spent whatever cash they got from whatever the hell they did for money, on the girls who ground their pussies and asses against poles for singles, fivers or the occasional lucky ten bucks.

Viktor tried to grab her arm as she breezed past him. "Jenna, baby come sit on my lap, I got a present for you!" Viktor slurred, his vodka bottle collection growing by the half-hour.

She knew he was already drunk to the point of not even being capable of keeping it up. Another one or two, and he'd probably be pissing himself. It would be up to the bouncers to drag his sorry drunken Russian ass out of the place for the umpteenth time before he staggered back in.

She truly hated this place, but it paid her bills and tuition. She lived simply, but it was enough to scrape by without having to work three waitressing jobs, like some of her friends, and study.

"Sorry Viktor, I gotta go see Dimitri, maybe some other time I'll give you a lap dance hey?" She winked as she peeled his hand from her.

"Free of charge?" Viktor asked hopefully.

"Uh-uh, sorry honey, I don't do freebies."

Viktor cursed her in Russian. She knew a lot of foreign swear words from her time here. She pulled free of his grasp and continued on her fury-fuelled journey across the stained carpet that alternated between stiff-and-sticky.

She knocked on the door to the office, heard a voice call something out and opened it to find Dimitri balls deep in Savannah.

"Oh shit, sorry." She turned to leave.

"No, no, it's fine." Dimitri motioned her into his office while pounding harder into a moaning Savannah.

Jenna felt awkward, the last thing she wanted to see was her boss fucking one of her co-workers. That was a hard limit for her. Each time he'd invited her into his office for a 'talk' he had asked her to lay on his desk so he could fuck her. She had refused every time. He had even insulted her by offering her money for the pleasure of him pleasuring her.

Jenna might have been a stripper, but she had standards. "Uh, I can come back." She half turned and pointed to the door. She hoped he would let her go, but there was no such luck.

"Almost… fucking... done…! Dimitri groaned as he came, slapping Savannah hard on her rump and she squealed. He pushed the girl forward and she fell to her hands and knees. After pulling her G-string back up around her ass, she trotted out, giving Jenna a wink as she passed. The door closed behind her, leaving Jenna and Dimitri alone.

"Jenna, baby, alone in my office, and I've already had a good fucking. You should have come in earlier, we could have had a good time. Yes?" He fisted his cock, still slick from Savanna's pussy and licked his lips.

Jenna felt the revulsion creep up her insides, she barely fought the urge to gag. She took a breath and shook her head, "That's not why I'm here, Dimitri, and you know it. You changed my roster again. I have classes and I can't do those shifts!" She crossed her arms over the skimpy outfit she wore, a single G-string with a sparkly matching bra. She felt self-conscious when she was alone with her boss, and even more so when she was wearing next to nothing. She would have been far more comfortable in jeans and t-shirt as opposed to what she had on now.

Dimitri shook his head. "Jenna, Jenna, Jenna." He stepped around the desk and perched on the corner, closer to her than she would have liked. "You work the shifts we give you and be thankful for it, yes? You know you can't pay for your college and your rent and your food and the fucking pretty clothes that you whores like to wear unless you fuck the poles and ride the laps of the fucking customers like a good slut."

Jenna flinched as Dimitri's voice grew louder and more aggressive with each word he spoke. He was nose to nose with her, and his spittle dampened her face.

He calmed himself and pulled back. "Besides, we have a very lucrative proposition for you girls, one you cannot refuse." He smirked.

"Now go, we have a staff meeting later tonight. After the shows finish, just after closing, everyone will be there." He cupped her chin with his fingers, slick and smelling of female musk. She shuddered inwardly knowing exactly where those fingers had been. "Now, go out there and get ready for your special show, baby." He lowered his lips to hers.

She pulled away, turning her head to the side as Dimitri's lips slid over her cheek, his tongue tasted her skin and he groaned. She shuddered as he let her go. No amount of hot showers would wash away his touch.

She turned and left his office, thudding into a solid mass of leather-clad muscle. She tilted her head and gazed into the bluest pair of eyes she had ever seen. She was stunned to see the handsome young face those eyes belonged to. Her balance wavered, she felt herself falling backward, but his hands captured her arms, holding her in place.

"You okay?" His words slid over her befuddled mind.

"Oh, uh… yes… ah, excuse me…" She sidled around the two bikers, her face flushed with embarrassment.

Within an hour, she was ready for her next show. The stage and poles beyond beckoned her. She peeked out through the bright stage lights and noticed the two bikers sitting at the bar. They chatted to Dimitri's brother, Vladimir, who was working the bar.

The handsome one, with the stunning eyes, watched her as she twirled around the pole, throwing her legs out and writhing her body against the friction-warmed metal.

If she was going to dance tonight, she would dance for one guy, and one guy only. Him.

Chapter Three

Firebird had to continuously adjust himself while in this place. Sure all the girls were pretty, but when *she* took the stage, he knew he had no hope of becoming flaccid. No amount of imagining unsexy things, such as Dagger's fat ass in a pair of short shorts, would do it. He nearly came in his pants when she grasped hold of the pole, climbed it and slid down it head-first, her legs spread and her G-string disappearing between the sweet round globes of her ass.

"Damn, wish I was the string of that thong." Tank clinked his beer against Firebirds.

Firebird nodded with a grunt of agreement. She was stunning, and she remained on his mind from the moment he had bumped into her in the hall outside Dimitri's office.

"Who?" Vladimir glanced at the stage. "Oh Jenna, the Australian girl? Yes, good luck getting her to spread her legs. I've been trying for about two years, since she came here. She is a woman who knows how to keep your cock hard, but never lets you dip in the pool, you know what I am saying?"

Firebird grunted, he wasn't sure if he wanted to get involved with a stripper, but if he ever did, he knew it would be Jenna.

"So, we were told to come here, and work security for you guys. In return, your boss and our club will have a lucrative business deal?"

Vladimir nodded. "Da, that's how it works. The details are not important, but it will be very good business for us all. Plus, you boys get to enjoy a free show, on the house, maybe even one of the girls take you out back and suck your cocks."

Tank grinned. "Now that's a sweetener to the deal."

Firebird's eyes were riveted on the luscious Jenna. She seemed to be dancing just for him. Her eyes locked onto his. Her body made love to the pole, her hips gyrated with a natural flow and she owned the stage. Moving to the beat of the music, but not in a jerky motion like the other two dancers who had taken up poles behind her. No, she was a natural. Firebird found himself hooked, watching her until she finished, bills stuck in the tight waistband of her G-string, as she sashayed off stage and the next group of strippers came on to hump poles and shake their asses to the catcalls and lewd comments from the patrons as the music pumped around them

Her presence on stage was missed when she finished, but to Firebird's pleasant surprise, she came out to the main floor to 'mingle' with the customers, not that there were too many around. She was wearing a little more, though it was still less than you'd wear out in public. A lace teddy hugged her body as she wandered towards them. She seemed to be free from harassment, as the other girls had found a customer to entice to the VIP area for some 'one-on-one' dancing. Jenna slipped up to the bar where Firebird was keeping an eye on the floor, Tank had gone to stand guard at the VIP area, where the girls were grinding over the laps of their customers.

Firebird nodded to her as she came up and sat on a stool near him. Her perky breasts were covered by a red lace bra, and her sweet cheeks exposed via the G-string which barely covered her nether regions.

"Evening Miss, I didn't hurt you before did I?"

Jenna laughed, her voice musical and bright. "No, no, you didn't. I was just flustered. I don't like meeting with the boss on a good day. Dimitri… he's… well, scary at times." The new shift's bartender slid a bowl of peanuts over to him, and placed a glass of ice water in front of Jenna.

"Thanks Charlie." She smiled and blew the guy a kiss.

Firebird felt a flare of jealousy zing through his body as the bartender pretended to catch the blown kiss and stick it in the pocket of his jeans.

"How's that boyfriend of yours?" she asked the bartender. Her light Australian twang sounded sweet and sexy and drove sensual energy straight to his cock.

"Oh honey, he's fine. He's worried I'll turn straight with all this class-A pussy and titties being ground in my face." The man chuckled. "But then, when I have all this hunky man-meat in front of me, oh I do love a man in leathers!"

Firebird spat out his beer, it dribbled down the scruff of his stubble and the front of his shirt to dampen it to the point of transparency. His face flushed and he turned to glare at the bartender.

Jenna laughed, and put a hand on his arm, it seemed to calm him instantly. "It's okay, Charlie's just pulling your leg, he's in a committed relationship." She grinned, looking down at his beer-soaked shirt. "Come on, let's get you cleaned up. You don't look that respectable with beer soaking the front of your shirt." She took him by the arm and led him backstage to the dressing area. Tiffany was adjusting her bra, the sequins sparkling blue and purple as she shimmied into it.

"Lookin' Good Tiff." Jenna giggled and slapped Tiff on the butt as she sashayed past.

"Hey! Watch it, I don't need a handprint on my ass before Showtime."

"Oh, you love it." Jenna winked.

"You know me too well." Tiffany countered. "Who's the hot hunk of man here?" She eyed Firebird like a hungry predator.

"This is one of the new bouncers… and I was so rude that I didn't get your name…?" She turned from Tiffany to him.

"Brett, but you can call me Firebird."

"Ooh 'Brett but you can call me Firebird' That's cute." Tiff adjusted her oversized tits. The sequins sparkled in the lights again and she grinned. "Well, have fun you two, and be done before we're finished, I don't want to see you going at it like rabbits when I get off stage."

Jenna barked a short laugh. "Tiff, you know I'm not like Savannah, slut of the jungle." She pulled out a chair and beckoned Firebird to sit down.

"Don't let her hear you say that; it may be true, but she'll bitch slap you into next Tuesday, honey." Tiff said as the cues for her entry onto stage began to play. "Shit, I'm on, Catch you later, Firebird." Tiff left the dressing room and dashed out towards the stage area.

"She's… nice," Firebird said carefully.

"Yeah, Tiff's all right."

"So, you're from Australia.?"

"Born here, in New York. My Daddy was in the US Army and got posted over to Australia where he met my Mum. Dad moved back to the states with rotation, Mum followed him, with me inside her. I have a double residency, or is it citizenship? One of the two, always get them confused." She leaned against the bench where all her makeup was sitting and perused his body.

"So why do you work here?" he asked her. She smiled at him as she grabbed some cleansing wipes and dabbed the dribbles of beer which stained his jaw.

"I'm working to pay for my college tuition. 'stripping for college'. Cliché I know, but it pays the bills and keeps me fed and studying." She scrunched up the wipes, tossing them into the bin.

His face felt a lot cleaner. She looked back at him, her hands on her hips and a cheeky smile on her face. He could look at that beautiful face for hours, kiss those lips for days, and make love to that body of hers for weeks.

"Let's get you cleaned up. Shirt off." She nodded to his shirt.

Firebird grinned and pulled his cut from his shoulders so he could remove his shirt. It was soaked with beer and stank.

Jenna watched as he pulled the shirt over his head and wolf whistled.

Firebird chuckled. He knew he was built, he worked out almost every day.

***

"Well, fuck me." Jenna said under her breath as she ogled his muscles. On his chest, over his heart was a small tattoo of a Phoenix, in full flight and ablaze. Her index finger trailed over the intricate ink work decorating his skin. On the other side, were the words *"Ride free"* inked in blue. Her fingers trembled as she traced those words.

One day, she would love to be able to ride free. Free of this place. Free of Dimitri's attempts to get her to fuck him. Free of the leering bastards who paid a pittance to see her shake her ass and tits on stage. But, that day was a very long way off.

"Is that an invitation, or a demand?" He grinned as he stood up and handed her his soiled shirt. He towered over Jenna, her eyes widened and her breath heaved in short pants as he leaned over her.

Their attraction was undeniable. He leaned down slowly, his intentions clear. Her mouth called him to kiss her, those soft lips waiting for his to touch her. They were so close, he could feel the heat of her breath tickling his stubble, warming his own lips.

"Firebird! Get the fuck out here!" He heard Tank's desperate voice shouting from the main room.

"Fuck." Firebird pulled his cut back over his shoulders, knowing he had to answer his brother's call. He reluctantly pulled away from Jenna, glancing back at her as he walked. "I'll be back, soon," he promised as he left to deal with a fight that had broken out over one of the girls. Shouts, and girlish screams were heard from beyond the backstage curtain.

When he had left, Jenna sucked in a deep breath.

"Holy shit, what the fuck was that?" She turned and looked into the mirror, leaning on her hands. Her skin was deliciously flushed and her eyes sparkled, if she didn't know better, she might have thought she'd had an orgasm right there. It damn near came close, even without him touching her.

No man had ever had that effect on her before. This was all too much, she had to go. She was off the clock and didn't really need to be here, other than the meeting, but she could catch up with one of the girls later that week and find out what it was all about. She put Firebird's beer-soaked shirt into a plastic bag before she put it into her backpack, quickly changed into a more comfortable jeans and tee-shirt number and headed home.

***

Firebird entered the dressing room soon after breaking up the fight between two drunken patrons to find a woman in leopard print lingerie preparing for her show.

"Hey, is Jenna in here?" he asked the woman. She continued to preen in front of the mirror before she replied.

"Oh, Jenna went home, she's finished for the day, but I'm here baby. I'm Savannah. I'm sure I can… help you with whatever you need." She looked him up and down, eyeing the slight bulge in his crotch. Her hand reached out and gave his package a squeeze. "Oh I'm certain I can help you with that." She rubbed his cock into a full erection.

Firebird grinned. "Sorry baby." He grasped her hand and pulled it from his crotch, "I gotta finish work first, then I gotta get back to my club."

"Some other time then?" Savannah said. "But here's a parting gift." She took his hand and placed it on her satin-covered tits. Firebird groaned, his cock even harder now. "We can always pick up where we left off another day." She winked as she pulled away, her hard nipples showing through the thin satiny material. "Thanks for the perk-up, baby." She said with a wink.

Firebird grinned and left the dressing room, adjusting himself as he went.

Though Savannah's touch had affected him, it was Jenna who was on his mind.

Chapter Four

Jenna looked over her textbooks, she sighed, it was no use. Her concentration was shot. She glanced at the neatly folded and laundered shirt. Firebird's shirt.

She had a few days off now, and wouldn't be back at the strip club for work until Thursday, when things started to get busy for the Russian brothers coming up to the weekend.

Jenna sighed. She could take the shirt back to Firebird via his clubhouse on the way to her class tonight. She sighed, thinking about the hard planes of his muscled body caused her body to tingle in such a way that not even her BOB could satisfy her. Those blue eyes had haunted her every waking moment.

"You can't fall for him," Jenna admonished herself. "He's a bad boy." Slipping the end of her pen into her mouth, she chewed on it, mangling the plastic with her front teeth. She sighed and decided to take a quick shower and cook something for dinner before class.

Jenna showered, and dressed in a sensible pair of jeans and a long-sleeved shirt which showed a little cleavage. She fixed her hair and headed out to her trusty but rusty hatchback.

The drive to the Maelstrom compound was accompanied by the sounds of the Red Hot Chilli Peppers blasting through her car stereo. She turned the stereo off when she pulled up out front of the compound. A trucking company was next door, and she could see men in leather vests like Firebird's working around the trucks.

Jenna waited for a moment getting the courage to approach the front gate, where two men were watching her.

"Okay, let's get this done with." She killed the engine as she opened the door before all courage failed her and she drove off. She stepped out, her heels crunching on the gravel road. The men leaned casually against the cyclone fence, eying her as she approached.

"What can we do for you, miss?" the larger one asked.

"Uh, Firebird left his shirt at the club, I washed it. Can you give it back to him for me please?" The guy grinned, and opened the gate.

"You know what? Why don't you go on in and give it to him yourself?" the other man nodded.

Jenna looked from one to the other. "Are you sure? I mean I don't want to intrude; I'm just dropping his shirt off."

"Yeah, 'Bird should be in the main room, just go through the door you'll see him."

Jenna walked toward the concrete walls of the clubhouse, the sounds of loud music playing within was muffled as she walked past row after row of shiny motorcycles. She opened the door and was assaulted by the sounds, sights and scents of a full-blown biker party.

Naked women writhed in the laps of the men, or were bent over the pool table, while others bobbed their heads over the laps of the men. It was basically a booze-fuelled sex party and despite the fact that Jenna worked in a strip club, this was all a little too much for her. She noticed one chick snorting a line of cocaine from a table, while she was taken from behind by one large and fat biker, the powder spilling over the table and smearing over her face when he thrust hard into her.

She quickly looked around and spotted Firebird. With a naked Redhead's face buried in his crotch. Jenna sighed, she felt hurt, but knew it was stupid to feel that way. She strode past the bodies on the couches, stepping over two chicks who were eating each other out on the floor and stopped in front of Firebird.

"Hey, sorry to interrupt, but here's your shirt." She dropped it on the seat beside him.

Firebird looked up at her, his jaw dropped, and the look on his face would have been priceless if not for the moaning of the redhead as she fingered herself while her lips were sucking his cock.

"Jenna." His face paled as if he had been caught doing something wrong.

"It's okay, I'll see you at work." She turned before he could see the tears fall from her eyes. She tried to hold her face in a mask, only managing to hold back the tears before she got back to her car. They fell freely as she drove off to her night class, not noticing the silhouette of Firebird standing in the street behind her car as she drove away from the clubhouse.

***

Firebird watched as the taillights of her little car drew away from him. He had seen the look in her eyes, though it shouldn't have mattered. It felt like a knife in his chest. They weren't together, though he knew that she could be his, if only he asked.

He knew he wanted her, tonight had cemented that fact. He pulled the zipper up on his jeans and headed back inside, ignoring the club party in full swing, ignoring the club whores who tried to get his attention, and ignoring the two chicks eating each other out on the carpet. Instead he picked up his shirt, leaving Red to finish off one of his brothers, and headed up to his room.

He flopped down on his unmade bed and put the shirt to his face. The scent of her washing powder brought him images of Jenna. Her long hair down, her deep brown eyes watching him as she traced the ink on his chest. Her perky tits, and sweet ass that was just big enough for him to handle. He groaned as his cock hardened.

He slid the zipper of his jeans down and gripped himself, stroking and smearing the lipstick Red had left on his cock. His stroked himself to thoughts of Jenna's pert lips covering his cock, her tongue stroking over his shaft as he gently ran his fingers through her long dark strands. Faster he stroked himself, pushing toward his climax. He groaned again, feeling his seed spurt from the tip of his cock to cover his hands.

"Fuck," he moaned. He knew he would have to do something about this Jenna situation. He'd have to make it up to her somehow. He got to his feet and washed up in the communal bathroom, the noise of the party hadn't abated.

Firebird decided he needed some space, his Harley beckoned. He checked out with the two guys on the gate, letting them know he was going for a ride. Killjoy chuckled at him, saying something about finding the hot little number who had his shirt. Firebird laughed, but wanted to punch Killjoy in the mouth for speaking about his Jenna.

His Jenna. Firebird liked the sound of that. His lips curled into a grin as he pulled his helmet on and kicked the engine over. He rode from the compound and out to clear his head and do some thinking.

Chapter Five

"We missed you at the staff meeting, Jenna." Dimitri's voice purred just behind her ear, his breath pushing errant strands of her hair, tickling the shell. She unconsciously reached back to push her hair back behind her ear.

"Sorry Dimitri, I didn't feel well and I had to get home." She reached for her mascara.

"Well, it's all right. I'm sure you'll catch up with what's going on later tonight."

Jenna looked up as she applied the mascara to her lashes, Dimitri's smirk caught in the reflection of the mirror. She scowled as he walked away before she finished getting herself ready.

She hadn't seen Firebird since she had dropped his shirt off at the clubhouse, Tank had been on bouncer duty for the last couple of days, and he had smiled kindly at her, but nothing had been said. He seemed to be the strong, silent type. The kind you had to be careful of because you didn't know if he was going to simply smile at you in a friendly way, or smile as he punched you if you crossed him.

The spotlight beamed down on her as she stepped onto the stage. Tiffany and Stella were already grinding themselves against their poles, while hers awaited at the end of the T-shaped stage. There was a large crowd in attendance, several well-dressed men were being personally attended to with drinks by Dimitri and Vladimir.

Jenna watched as they schmoozed with their customers. She suspected her employers were involved in a Russian crime syndicate but she didn't want to know the nitty-gritty details. All she was concerned with was her weekly paycheck, and the tips from the customers which kept her fed, clothed, and a roof over her head.

She gripped the pole and began to work her body around it, sliding against the slim, smooth metal which had borne hundreds of other exotic dancers before her, and would host many more after her. She was thankful the damned things were sanitised every night, who knew what little bugs would be found lurking on the metal.

She whipped her head back and forth as the music pulsed through her body like a lover's touch, arching her body backward to poke her tits out to the catcalls and hoots of appreciation from the men before she pulled herself back up, flush with the pole. She lowered herself into a crouch, her legs spreading at the knees, giving the horny men a good look at what she was working before she moved quickly, standing up and lifting a leg high above her head, curling it back and using the bent leg as an anchor to twirl around the pole.

The music pulsed through her as she danced, shifting closer to the edge of the stage, where she got to her hands and knees, letting the men pull the waistband of her G-string and slide notes inside. She felt a few solid spanks on her ass cheeks and a couple of well-placed gropes. She tried to ignore the manhandling, but still felt revulsion. This was the part of the job she hated.

This was not what her father would have had her do, but he was back in Minnesota, preparing to move back to Australia with her mom. Blissfully ignorant of what his beloved daughter was doing to support herself.

Her show finished, and she and the girls cleaned themselves up in preparation to head onto the floor to mingle with customers. She hated this part, she hated having to give lap dances to fat men who tipped like shit, all so they could get their grubby paws on a woman who wasn't their wife.

She sashayed through the open floor seating area, smiling and flirting with the customers, trying to snag someone for a quick lap dance, but tonight no-one seemed interested, until Dimitri beckoned her over.

"Jenna." He smiled, pulling her against him, his hand splayed over her hip. She smiled saccharinely as his hand pulled up the satiny material of her teddy, exposing her hip. He returned his hand to her skin, tracing patterns with his fingers. Her gut churned at his touch.

Before them, in a curved booth sat three men, all dressed in suits. Two others stood by, obviously bodyguards for the men.

"This is Mr. Balakin, Mr. Veselov, and my uncle, Kazimir Rodchenko." He seemed quite proud to be related to the last man.

Jenna smiled and nodded to each man. "Good evening, Gentlemen." She nodded to each in turn, and offered a sweet smile she didn't feel.

"Jenna, my uncle has expressed an interest in your entertaining him this evening. You and he should head to the VIP room to get *acquainted*." He smiled.

Jenna felt as if the air had been sucked from the room. She felt Dimitri's fingers dig into her hips when he felt her balk at the mention of them being *acquainted*.

She smiled thinly, and nodded. "Of course, Dimitri." She held her hand out to Mr. Rodchenko. He smiled, showing the gold rimming his two front teeth. He leaned forward and took her hand, standing up. The man towered over her. He took her by the arm, releasing her hand as he and the two bodyguards followed them to the stairs leading to the VIP room.

Tank stood guard at the door to the VIP room. He nodded in greeting and opened the room, letting them in. Mr. Rodchenko handed him a hundred-dollar bill.

"You can go now, I'm sure my nephews need you downstairs to keep an eye on the common rabble." His accent was heavy and his grip tightened on Jenna's arm.

Tank's eyes flicked to Jenna's face, he could tell there was a deep-seated fear hidden behind the mask she kept on her face.

***

Rodchenko was a dangerous man. The man's reputation for violence preceded him. Tank was aware of the MC's agreement with the Russians. They trucked the drugs and weapons the Russians sold, and were given access to the strip club and its girls as well as payments of cash for the club's coffers. The Club had voted, and agreed to let their members work as security for the club, an offer made by the Russians which benefited the club as they got a reduced price for weapons bought off the Russians.

Tank sighed, as the two goons Rodchenko brought up with him took their places on either side of the door. There was nothing for it, but to head downstairs and work the floor. He passed Dimitri on the way down.

"You've been reassigned; you work the door now." He muttered as he lit up a cigarette.

Tank nodded, his thoughts on the fear shining clearly in the girl's eyes but hidden deep within her mask. Firebird was interested in her; Tank knew this. But, he knew it was the girl's job to work in this shithole, and she had to make her money somehow. He hadn't thought she would allow herself to go through with what Rodchenko and Dimitri had planned.

He took his place outside the front door with one of the other brothers who was working, bummed a smoke and watched as his expertly blown smoke rings were illuminated by the light from the overhead hot pink neon lights.

Chapter Six

Jenna looked at the room, it had been completely transformed from what she remembered, gone were the threadbare and cum-stained chairs set around a small area where the girls would dance privately for their clients. There was a two-way mirror making up one wall. The view from it showed the floor below, the women dancing on poles and the men waving money to entice the girls to dance closer to them.

She turned and noticed the single pole and small circular stage, that wasn't new, but the stage had been re-surfaced, a reflective mirror made up the floor of the stage, and the pole had been gold plated. The room was painted in reds and blacks, with four small stage lights shining above the pole.

A bed was placed in a corner, the red satin sheets, shone with a dark promise of what was to come. But what really shocked Jenna, was the addition of three video cameras, and men to work them.

Vladimir smiled when she saw him. He loaded a tape into one of the cameras and shut the cover with a snap. "Ah, Jenna, about time we got you in here. Mr. Rodchenko was quite adamant you were to be his first.".

Dimitri entered, his face twisted into a leering smile. "Is she ready?" he asked.

Mr. Rodchenko sat in the Queen Anne-style armchair, a table filled with cigar boxes and full liquor bottles sat beside it

"If she's not, she soon will be." The Russian crime boss smiled. He indicated for Jenna to take the stage while the men aimed their cameras towards her.

"Dance for me, pretty girl." He lit a cigar and poured himself some scotch from a bottle that looked to be top-shelf stuff.

Through the room's speakers, erotic music began to play, the lights above the stage came on, bathing her in shades of red. Jenna swallowed the nervous bile threatening to force its way up her throat. This was not something she was willing to do, yet she knew she had no choice. The looks Dimitri and his brother were shooting at her, told her in no uncertain terms, she couldn't refuse to do anything Rodchenko told her to do.

She moved to the small stage, her hands gripping the pole as she hoisted herself onto the smooth mirrored surface. Her body moved stiffly at first, her mind racing to try to find a way out of this, knowing the final outcome would be with her on the bed, Rodchenko's large and somewhat tubby body covering hers.

She swallowed the bile again, fighting the tears that threatened to ruin her carefully applied mascara as she began to dance for Rodchenko.

Her body movements changed as her mind slipped to a place where she felt safe. Firebird's face replaced that of Rodchenko's, and she danced not for the Russian, but for Firebird.

Her body moved sensually, teasing the men in the room with her fluidity of movement, the raw sexual prowess she exuded, safe on the stage. She ignored the red blinking lights of the camera as she removed her teddy, dancing in her bra and G-string. Soon she removed her bra, exposing her natural beauty to the hungry eyes of the men in the room. With just her G-string on, the man seated before her began panting for her body like a dog after a bitch in heat.

She wished that it was Firebird sitting in the chair, and not the man who, at a snap of his fingers, could have her rotting in a ditch.

The music softened in volume as Rodchenko leaned back in his chair, beckoning her to leave the stage and come to him. She stepped down from the stage and moved towards him. He pulled her down onto his lap, her legs either side of his knees. He lifted his hips, grinding his erection against her. His moan vibrated through his body as his hands gripped her hips. Her breasts before the rough stubble of his face, his breath heating the skin in an uncomfortable way.

Jenna trembled, her body reacting to the fear she felt. She didn't want to be here. Rodchenko's hands coaxed her to move against him. She rubbed her body against him, hearing his moans as she moved faster and harder, grinding herself against him. She felt dirty, disgusting and hated every moment of this impromptu lap dance.

She forced herself to put her arms around Rodchenko's neck, her eyes on Dimitri who stood behind them, watching as Rodchenko nuzzled against her neck and she rocked against him. The cameras red lights blinked on and off as they recorded every movement she made against the older man.

He gripped her ass and hoisted her up as he stood, a hand going to fumble with his belt. Jenna felt Rodchenko's suit pants fall down to his ankles, his bare skin and hard cock pressing against her.

He carried her over to the bed, throwing her face down into the covers. Her heart beat wildly in her chest as she tried to scramble to get away from him, the nightmare taking a desperate turn for the worst.

"I love it when they struggle." Rodchenko muttered. He pulled his belt from his pants and gripped her wrists, tying them together with his belt. His hands went to her panties and she felt them being ripped from her hips. Cool air met bare skin. Jenna whimpered as she felt him press himself against her entrance, she closed her eyes as she felt him enter her. Hot tears fell from her closed lids as the Russian took her while her bosses filmed every heartbreaking moment of it.

When it was all over, Jenna curled up on the bed, ignored by the men who congratulated each other on a good film. A tight roll of fifties landed beside her. There was a thousand dollars sitting by her curled up body. Dimitri came and sat on the bed beside her, his hands stroking over her trembling and abused flesh.

"Now, you realise that you should have come to the meeting, yes?" He picked up the roll of notes, pulling several hundred dollars out before he tossed the rest of them onto the bed beside her.

"This is going to happen a lot more often, it's a good way to make money, and some of our richer clients want to become porn stars with our girls." He leaned in and kissed her on the cheek. "You are going to be a star, Jenna." His rancid breath assaulted her nose.

"Get dressed, then get your ass back out onto the floor." He raised his hand and slapped her ass so hard that she screamed. She knew there would be a large, red handprint on that cheek, exposed for all to see when she went up on stage. She was left alone in the room, the cameras now silent, their red lights dark. The soft music continued to play as she got her teddy and bra back on, her ruined panties she left hanging on the armrest of the chair. She stepped out of the VIP room to find the hallway was empty. She held her head down as she made her way through the crowds, thankful that people continued to ignore her as she passed them.

Jenna made it to the dressing room where she cleaned the mascara which had smeared her cheeks. The woman who looked back at her in the reflection was a stranger, she didn't recognise herself.

Her eyes were haunted, her lips swollen from forced kisses, and a bruise under her eye was darkening from the sudden punch that Rodchenko had gifted her with when he climaxed, spilling his seed inside her. She was thankful she was on the pill, but it didn't stop her from heading to the shower to scrub herself over and over until her skin shone pink from the loofah.

She dried and dressed in a new lingerie set, sliding a satin teddy over her sore and abused body. She studied the red marks worn into her skin from Rodchenko's belt. His last words to her gave her goose bumps of dread,

"You and I will be seeing a lot more of each other, I think."

Chapter Seven

"Man, I tell ya, something was off with Jenna last night." Firebird said as he sat at the club's bar, a cold beer in his hands and the sounds of the jukebox playing old rock. Around them, the club whores were sitting with the brothers, some headed up to the rooms, others playing pool or just talking with the men.

Firebird's father was talking with the V.P. their voices hushed as they kept their heads together in conversation.

"What makes you think that?" Tank asked him.

It had been a week since Firebird had last seen Jenna. She had been on his mind the whole time he was on the ride out, keeping the Russian iron, that their trucking company transported, protected on their cross-country journey. He had returned the night before, and had worked the day shift at the strip club. Jenna had been quiet, not her usual bubbly self. Firebird was due to go back there for the late shift.

"Not sure, but she wouldn't look me in the eye. I think it had something to do with the party we had about a week back. She brought my shirt in, sweetheart had washed it and brought it back to me, but she caught me getting a blowjob from Red." He tilted the bottle to his lips and took a swig.

"You got a thing for the luscious Jenna?" Tank asked him, before he took a swig of his own beer.

Firebird chuckled, playing with the edge of his beer bottle's label. "Yeah, I think I do. She's smart, gorgeous, got a great pair of tits, and an ass to die for. And, damned if I don't think her personality tops it off perfectly." Firebird peeled the label from the bottle and began to tear it into strips.

"So, ask her out," Tank suggested.

"You think I'm 'dating' material?" Firebird laughed. "Come on, Brother. Look at me. I'm a newly patched biker. I got no real job, other than what the club gets me to do. I technically still live with my parents, and I sleep with club whores. This life, it ain't for Jenna."

"Jenna isn't so innocent either." Tank turned toward his brother. "She's a stripper, she takes her shit off for money, lets men grope her, grind their dirty cocks against her, man."

"I never heard you complaining about getting a lap dance, or a blowjob from that girl, what's her name? Savannah? You know she's the club slut there right?" Firebird grinned. "Jenna's not the kinda girl that Savannah is, she's just trying to make her payments for college."

"Do you really know her that well?" Tank asked him.

Firebird narrowed his eyes at Tank. "Brother, I like the girl. I'd like to know her better than I already do. I'll take your advice. I'm going to ask her out, if she says no, then she says no."

"Well, good luck, brother." Tank shrugged. The way he said it made Firebird's *bump for trouble* itch.

"There something I ought to know about regarding Jenna, brother?" Firebird asked Tank.

"That might be up to her to tell you if there is. I haven't touched her."

Firebird nodded, but he knew there was something Tank and Jenna weren't telling him. She had been so comfortable with him when they first met. The fire that seemed to blaze between them drew them closer to each other. He wanted to feel that burn again.

He downed his drink and headed up to his room to rest and shower before his shift.

***

The lights and noise of the strip club hadn't changed, but the atmosphere around the girls had changed considerably. There was an element of something in the air. The looks in the girl's eyes showed something… fear.

Jenna was up on stage, dancing. Her body moving to the flow of the music, her hands gripping the sweat-covered pole as she swung around it like a pro-gymnast-gone-stripper. Firebird could see the sweat trickling down her back as she worked under the heat of the lights. He caught her eyes and noticed the lack of emotion in them, almost like she had lost an important part of herself.

He frowned, wondering what the hell had happened while he was gone the last week.

Dimitri beckoned him over. "I want you to work the door after eight, we have important clients arriving and we need tight security on the doors to keep the drunks out." Dimitri pulled a packet of cigarettes from his pocket, he offered one to Firebird, who took it and lit Dimitri's before he fired up his own.

Dimitri smiled at him. "You do good work, Firebird, you will go far in your organisation, and we might have more work for you, if your father lets you off the chain once in a while." Dimitri patted Firebird on the back.

"My loyalties lie with the MC, Dimitri." Firebird pulled the cigarette from his mouth and casually blew the smoke away from the Russian. "Long as I am told to work here, then here's where I'll be." He slid the cigarette back between his lips and grinned. "So, on the door at eight right?"

Dimitri nodded. "Yes, door at eight, until then go have drink on me, enjoy the show. The girls are working extra hard tonight; my uncle is coming. He is the VIP."

"I've seen him when he had a meeting with the Prez. Never met the man properly, though. Not my place to." Firebird said. "Right, back to it then." He stubbed the cigarette out in an ashtray before he headed to the bar where Charlie was serving.

"Hey stud," the bartender greeted him. "Ready to come to the wild side?" He popped the cap off the beer bottle and slid it to Firebird with a wink.

"Sorry, you're not my type. Not a sausage man." He grinned. "Jenna, however…" He turned to see her expertly swinging around the pole, her legs splitting as she twirled around it.

"Does Jenna seem different to you lately?" Firebird asked as he noticed her finishing up on stage.

"Different? Like how?" Charlie asked as he stocked up a few bottles on the shelf behind the bar.

"Quieter, withdrawn. Maybe a little…" Firebird was trying to find the right word.

"Bitchy? Oh she gets like that at *that* time of the month sweetie. All the girls do, I swear they all turn that bitch switch on at the same time, just to piss the boys off." Charlie chuckled. "Mine's on all the time though, so I don't often notice so much."

Firebird shook his head slightly, it didn't seem like that was the problem, but he couldn't be certain, and no way in hell was he going to ask if her *Aunt Flo* was visiting. Asking a woman something along those lines would most definitely end up with him on the ground clutching his most prized possession in agony.

Chapter Eight

Dimitri was there to escort her to the VIP room at eight o'clock on the dot.

"Ahh, Jenna, looking delicious as always."

"Dimitri, I don't want to do this." She pleaded. "Please, ask one of the other girls to do it, I'm sure Savannah…" she was cut off by Dimitri, shoving her back against the wall. The framed pictures of girls dancing naked on the poles rattled against the drywall with her impact. She gasped as she felt Dimitri's hand snake around her throat and clench tight.

"Savannah isn't here, bitch, she's no longer with us. She refused my uncle and now she's gone," Dimitri said, with an evil smirk. "Do you want to be next, Jenna? Do you want to *go away* as well?" The threat was veiled, but sincere. Jenna had a dark inkling as to exactly what Dimitri meant. She swallowed thickly, the action made difficult with Dimitri's hand clasped tight around her throat.

She blinked the tears away and shook her head. "No." she croaked.

Dimitri leaned forward and kissed her cheek, catching one of her tears on his lips. He pulled away, licking the salty teardrop. "Smart girl, now if you behave, you will get a little something extra later." He gripped her arm and led her down to the floor. She put on a fake smile for show while Dimitri kept his face passive as he took her through to the stairs leading to the VIP room.

The door opened and Rodchenko turned. He had been watching their approach. "Ahh, good evening my sweet Jenna, tonight you'll be entertaining not only me, but my two associates as well, you remember them? Mr. Balakin, and Mr. Veselov. Say hello to my sweet Jenna." He smirked as the men advanced toward her. "She likes it a little rough."

Jenna tried to pull back, but Dimitri's iron grip held her fast until the two men took her from him. She screamed, fighting them until Rodchenko stepped up and slapped her hard across the face.

"You shouldn't be rude to our guests, Jenna." He gripped her chin. "Now, are you going to be a good girl? Or do we need to make a film with you like we did of Savannah?"

She looked confused.

"So much blood, such a mess to clean up, but the video sold so very well." He laughed.

Jenna felt sick, lowered her head and surrendered.

"I'll behave, sir." She whispered when Rodchenko tilted her chin up to him.

"Good, I'd hate to destroy such a beautiful body." He put a cigar to his lips and lit up. The flame of his flip-lighter lit his face up like a demon.

"Roll the cameras!" he shouted.

***

Firebird and Smokey, one of his MC brothers stood by the door. Two hours after they had arrived, the VIPs departed. Their Russian words lost on Firebird. Dimitri called him back in to work the floor, now their VIPs had left, he seemed to be more relaxed.

Firebird worked security on the floor for another hour before he slipped out the back for a cigarette.

He stood beneath the single light, watching the moths as they fluttered about, attracted to the glowing globe above his head. He puffed away, blowing smoke and thinking about a beautiful stripper when she opened the door and stepped out, a silk dressing gown wrapped tightly around her.

"Hey." He said with a smile.

She ducked her head. "Oh, Sorry, I didn't mean to disturb you."

Firebird grabbed the door before she could close it.

"Hey, come on out, it's fine." He waited until she timidly stepped out onto the concrete step. "Haven't seen you for a while." He couldn't help noticing her change in behavior, and it wasn't for the better.

"Yeah, I've been here, you haven't." It almost sounded like an accusation. She reached over and pulled his packet of smokes from his top pocket, withdrew one and stuck it in her mouth. She snatched the silver lighter from his hand and tried unsuccessfully to light her cigarette. Firebird noticed her hands shaking.

"Jenna." He attempted to get her attention over the clicking of his flip lighter.

Click

"Jenna…"

Click

"Jenna…" the sparks of the flint from the lighter illuminated her face

Click, click, click-click-click-click "FUCK!" she screamed and threw the lighter into the night.

She stood, her chest heaving as she breathed deep and fast. Firebird sighed, taking the cigarette out of her mouth and lighting it with the end of his own. He put the freshly lit smoke back between her lips, holding it there while she puffed shallowly on it, tears falling down her cheeks. His eyes searched her beautiful face, noticing the slight blemishes she had tried to hide with make-up – were they bruises? Firebird's body tensed slightly. Maybe she had a boyfriend who was abusing her? If she did, he would find the asshole and put him in a ditch somewhere in the middle of nowhere.

"Rough night?" he asked her, his face etched with concern.

She reached up and took the cigarette from him. "Yeah." She wiped at the corners of her eyes and sniffled. "You could say it's been a rough week." She hugged her arms around herself.

"What are you doing after work? We could go get a cup of coffee at the diner on Holt Street."

Jenna stopped him, raising her hand in a stopping gesture, the fine smoke from the cigarette wisping skywards. "Firebird, I'm not looking for a date right now, I'm not looking for a one-night stand, a quick screw against the wall, or a boyfriend."

"Jenna, it's only coffee, and it's only as friends."
Firebird placed a reassuring hand on her shoulder. She
flinched, as if she had burned him and he pulled his hand
away .

"Sorry."

"Just coffee?"

He smiled and nodded. "Yeah, just coffee, and
maybe a slice of pie?"

"I like pie." She swiped at a stray tear away.

"Yeah, me too, my Mom makes a kickass pecan
pie." He suddenly felt decidedly hungry for his mother's
famous dessert. "So, is it a date? I can't guarantee the pie
will be as good as my Mom's, but they do make a good
cup of coffee."

"It's not a date, it's an outing with a friend."

Firebird smiled warmly, he saw a spark of the
Jenna he'd first met flaring back to life in her eyes.

"Awesome." He crushed his cigarette out with
his boot. "I'll meet you by the back entry when you get
off. You have jeans and a long sleeved shirt?" he asked
her

"Yeah, why?"

"I didn't drive here, I rode."

Chapter Nine

Jenna glanced at the bike. She was dressed in her sneakers, jeans and a long sleeved shirt. Coincidentally, it was the same clothing she had worn when she'd gone by the clubhouse.

Firebird grinned and held out a helmet to her as well as his leather jacket, minus the cut he kept on. He fitted the helmet to her chin, making sure the strap was tight and the helmet secure. She seemed to tremble under his touch as he gently traced his finger along her jawline, enjoying the contact with her soft skin. He got on the bike and waited for Jenna to slide on behind him. She settled away from him. He turned and looked at her over his shoulder

"Baby, if you don't ride snug up with me, you're going to fall on your pretty ass as soon as we take off." He grabbed her hands and pulled her forward, until she was pressed tight against his back. The thought of her sweet pussy pressed against him, even if separated by layers of clothing, made him instantly hard.

Damnit, this is going to be a long ride. It was made even longer when he took off and she clutched her arms around his middle, holding on for dear life.

He felt her move with him as he slid around corners, riding through the quiet streets of town until they came to the all-night diner on the edge of town frequented by truckers and bikers alike.

He stepped off his bike and helped Jenna to her feet. She stumbled a little, unsteady after the ride. She clutched the front of his cut and looked up at him, her brown eyes gazing into his and again he felt the strong magnetic pull of her. He smiled and helped her to stand upright.

"You okay?" he asked her. Jenna nodded as she unclipped the helmet. He took it from her and put it on the handlebars of his bike. "Okay, coffee and pie." He took her by the hand. She seemed to clutch his hand with a death grip as they entered the diner. Two groups of bikers were sitting and drinking coffee while a few scattered truckers were enjoying their break.

"Hey, Val," Firebird called out to the waitress.

"Brett, you're up awful early, or is it late?" the older woman grinned as she came over with an order pad.

"Late. Two coffees, and two slices of your best pie." He ordered as Val settled them in a booth.

Firebird clasped his hands in front of his mouth, leaning on his elbows he looked at Jenna. She seemed a little nervous. He put his hands down, realising he was unconsciously hiding behind them.

"Thanks for coming out with me, I wanted to apologise for anything you saw last week." He paused while Val poured them coffee and left to get their slices of pie.

"I know what I saw. It's okay, really. We're not going out, not together." Her voice revealed her sadness when she remembered what she'd seen in the clubhouse. Red's head bobbing up and down in his lap, his eyes rolled back as he rode the sensation of her mouth on his dick. The soft, illicit moans from his mouth that almost shattered her heart.

"Jenna, look, I really like you. There's something between us; I know there is." He leaned forward, placing his hand over hers. She was trembling.

"Firebird – Brett." She sighed. "I agree, there's something, but it can't come to anything." She spoke softly. "I'm not the person you need me to be. I'm not a club whore."

"Jenna, who said anything about you being a club whore?" Firebird looked at her as if she had two heads.

Val returned, placing plates of delicious-looking pie in front of them. "Anything else, sugar?" she asked.

Firebird shook his head. "No, that's all. Thanks."

He turned his gaze back to Jenna. "I want you, just you. I don't want to share you with anyone. I'd like to date you, exclusively."

"You'd like to date *me*?" Her voice rose with incredulity. "I'm a damned stripper, one tiny step away from actually being a whore." She held her thumb and forefinger an inch apart to demonstrate how close she was to crossing that line, little did Firebird know that she felt like that line had been crossed, last week, a roll of fifties tossed uncaringly beside her naked and trembling body was the nail in that particular coffin. "How the hell do you think that makes me *girlfriend* material?" Hearing her raised voice, one group of bikers turned and looked at him.

He recognised the V.P. of the Sons of Abaddon. The prick still had a score to settle with him over the torched car. Jenna stood and stormed from the diner, walking back toward the strip club, and her car.

Firebird sighed, squeezing the bridge of his nose with thumb and forefinger. There was definitely something amiss with Jenna. And now, he had to deal with the Sons of Abaddon as they stood up from their table with the scraping of chairs. Heavy booted footsteps approached him. The shadows of the four men who had watched Jenna leave with keen interest now darkened his table.

"Well, if it isn't *Firebird*, the little bastard who fucked my baby." A biker with the *V. President* patch on his cut sneered as he slid into the booth. He picked up Jenna's coffee and pie and downed them both. He chewed the pie open-mouthed and spat the globs of pastry and pie filling as he spoke. "We're going to teach you a lesson in manners, asshole." He said around a mouthful of pie.

"Manners?" Firebird laughed. "Didn't your mama tell you not to speak with your mouth full, asswipe?" He grimaced as he flicked a piece of saliva-doused pie from his cheek which had landed there after being launched from Johnny's mouth.

"I think you boys better move on out right now before I get real mad." Val's voice was accompanied by the sound of her cocking a 9mm. The V.P. of the Sons of Abaddon turned and eyed the older woman with a smirk.

"Okay Val, we'll leave." He knew better than to piss Val off. The local biker clubs in the area had a healthy respect for Val, and her diner was considered neutral ground.

"Good idea, Johnny. Take your shit elsewhere. I run a good, honest establishment and I expect to be respected, and my rules followed. No exceptions." Val kept the gun levelled on the men as they left the diner. She slipped the gun back in under her apron "I think you'd best head on back home as well, quick as you can, Firebird, no telling if Johnny will be waiting for you around the corner." She picked up his untouched pie. "I'll wrap this up to go." She removed the plate, disappeared into the kitchen and returned a moment later with a paper bag. "Give you father my regards." She escorted him out the door.

His bike was still there, untouched, though he made sure to check it thoroughly for sabotage. He wouldn't put it past the Sons of Abaddon to slash his tires, after all, he was on their shit list.

"Thanks, Val." He threw his leg over the tank of his bike and sat. He kicked the old bike to life and tore ass out of the parking lot.

He had gotten two blocks from the diner when he glanced in his mirrors and noticed lights coming up fast behind him. Firebird gunned the engine, taking an alleyway along the back of the main street. The roar of his engine was quadrupled by the arrival of his chasers. He gunned the engine harder, his hand twisting the throttle as he changed gears and accelerated.

He broke out through the end of the alley onto second street, narrowly missing one of the local garbage trucks. The driver stopped and shouted out at him, cursing as Firebird tore off down the alley opposite the one he burst through before the garbage truck moved forward again. Behind him he heard the screeching of tires and loud crunching as his hunters ended their ride in the side of the garbage truck.

Firebird didn't look back until he got to the compound. His father was outside, talking to their Sargent at Arms. "Hello Son, been out riding have we?"

"Yeah, took one of the girls from the strip club out for a coffee." Firebird answered as he took off his helmet and killed the engine on his bike.

"Come across any Sons of Abaddon in your travels?" his father asked, crossing his arms and raising an eyebrow in question

"Or did they join the sanitation company?" Dagger sniggered.

"I think the four of them might be nursing a few sore heads in the morning if they aren't in traction by then." Firebird grinned.

His father clapped him on the shoulder. "Go up and get some rest. Next time you go out, I want you to

take one of the brothers or one of the prospects with you.
I don't think this shit with the Sons of Abaddon is done,
not by a long shot."

Firebird nodded. "Got it Dad." He left his father
and Dagger to their business.

Chapter Ten

Jenna's allotted slot had finished, her sexy body sashayed off the stage. She seemed to be a little more reserved around him, and it irritated the shit out of Firebird. He had tried several times to talk to her, but she had withdrawn inside herself. Some of the other girls had done the same and he wondered what the hell was going on in this place.

Charlie was no help; the girls hadn't opened up to the gay bartender as they usually did. Firebird sighed as he scanned the floor for trouble. It was a quiet night, Wednesday. He was one of two bouncers at the club, the other, one of the prospects was working the door.

A group of men in leather cuts entered, Firebird was instantly on alert. He noted the plastered wounds on the face of one of the men, his arm in a cast and sling; it was one of the Sons of Abaddon who had chased him through the back alleys and ended up face planting the side of the garbage truck.

Firebird watched as the men drank, becoming more rowdy and grabby toward the passing girls as they became drunker.

Jenna passed wearing a teddy that hugged her sweet body in all the right places. Her forward motion was impeded by the meaty arm of one of the bikers as he reached out and grabbed her around the waist, hauling her into his lap.

She squealed and wriggled in his grip as he began to paw at her, his mouth pressing against the soft flesh of her neck while his brothers cheered him on and laughed at the struggling woman. Firebird's fury boiled over. He moved fast, pulled Jenna out of the guy's arms and let her step back before he rounded on the asshole who had mauled her, with a right hook that cracked against his jaw.

The club erupted in screams and shouts as more people joined the fray. Jenna ran back to the dressing room, the sounds of the brawl nipping at her heels.

"What the fuck is going on? Tiff's eyes widened in fright, her face pale against the bright red lipstick she had just applied. She stepped up to the door and looked out at the club

"Firebird punched a guy for grabbing me and all hell's broken loose."

Tiffany pulled aside the sequin-covered curtains, looking from the fray back to Jenna. "He did that for you?" She turned back to admire Firebird as he took on two more Abaddon boys, his fists flying. One went down, but another grabbed him from behind, pinning his arms and holding him secure while another got a few gut-punches in. Firebird seemed to go listless for a moment before he rallied, smashing his head back up into the nose of his captor.

A blood curdling scream heralded a spurt of red as the man's nose broke. Firebird wrenched free of the hold as the Son of Abaddon grabbed his bloody nose. The prospect entered the fray, leaping into battle with a high-pitched battle cry, that sounded suspiciously like a woman screaming.

Jenna and Tiffany watched as Firebird and the prospect got the upper hand. The Sons of Abaddon limped away when Dimitri intervened, his face a cloud of rage.

"What the fuck is going on here?" His voice was taut with anger.

Firebird wiped blood from a cut on his lip and glanced around. "A friendly disagreement on the treatment of your girls, Dimitri." Firebird grinned.

"This better not be one of your biker war incidents interfering with my club. If it happens again, you'll all be banned, and our arrangements will be at risk of being dissolved." Dimitri snarled, getting right into Firebird's personal space.

Firebird shrugged. "Don't worry, I wouldn't risk my club's association with you, not unless it came down from the Prez and VP." Firebird rubbed his thumb across his lip and winced at the sting.

Dimitri's breathing calmed slightly, though the force with which he expelled air through his nostrils sounded like an asthmatic bulldog with a cold. "Get yourself cleaned up, and put my club back in order. Now!" He spun on his heel and stormed back to his office.

The prospect patted Firebird on the shoulder. "I'll straighten up here, get your face cleaned up."

Firebird sighed, his face was starting to hurt like hell now the numbness was beginning to recede. He headed toward the dressing room where the first aid kit was stashed, noticing the movement of the curtain as someone moved away from it.

***

"So, you going to look after this or do you want me to?" Tiffany asked Jenna. "Because I'm so all for that!" Tiffany fanned herself.

"No, I'll get him." Jenna removed the first aid kit from under the dressing table. She shifted the makeup, titty tassels, discarded G-strings and bras from the table, tossing the underwear into the washing hamper where the girls should have tossed them once they were done. She heard Firebird's footsteps enter the dressing room behind her.

"Hey." She turned to him with a smile. His face resembled a battlefield. Bruises were blossoming on both cheeks, one eye was beginning to swell shut, and his lip was bleeding.

"Take a seat." She patted the seat cushion, stepping back so he could sit. She watched as he grimaced in pain. She dabbed antiseptic onto a cotton ball and pressed it against the split on his eyebrow with a look of concentration..

"Fuck, that shit stings!" He pulled away and attempted to stand.

Jenna placed her hand around his arm and held him still.

"Oh, you big baby." She tutted. "Big tough biker can't handle a little medical attention." She shook her head.

The almost-masculine clearing of a throat caught her attention before Firebird could retort.

"Hey sweetie, got your big hero here some ice." Charlie stepped in, holding a bag of ice wrapped in a tea towel. He smiled as he handed Jenna the ice pack.

"Thanks, honey." She grabbed Firebird's hand and forced him to hold the pack against his swelling eye.

Jenna continued to fix his injuries. "So, I'm now in your debt." She stepped back after she had finished patching him up.

"I owe you my thanks, for tonight and a thank you for the coffee the other night." Her eyes looked deep into his gorgeous blues. She turned, showing off her tight ass as she leaned forward and rummaged through her purse.

She retrieved a small, flat box, secured with a black bow. Harley Davidson logos peeked through the ribbon. Jenna leaned against the edge of the dressing room table as he locked eyes with her.

"You didn't have to get me anything. I think I was kind of a jerk the other night." His eyes drifted down to the box in his hands.

"No, I was a bitch, I've just… there's…" she stopped and sighed as if she was trying to find the right words, or at least the courage to continue. "I have a few things going on right now, and I don't think I'm ready to be dating anyone. I'm studying and trying to keep my job, my apartment and my course going. It's a juggling act and it's hard. But, I'm getting there. I'm just not stable enough for a romance right now." She nodded to the gift box in his hands.

"Open it. I owe you this." She crossed her arms over her chest, which encouraged her breasts to perk up in the teddy she still wore.

Firebird was forced to endure yet another Jenna-induced erection. He shifted in the seat, crossing one leg over the other to try to hide the bulge in his pants. She blushed, and he knew he'd been caught out.

The lid of the box came off, and he removed black tissue paper. Nestled within was a silver-plated flip lighter with the Harley Davidson logo. Firebird grinned as he took out the lighter. "Damn, this is beautiful." He looked up at her, his appreciation for both his gift and for her shone from his eyes. "Thank you, Jenna."

"You're welcome. I'm sorry I tossed your other lighter." She sighed. "I'd better get back out there. Are you all right to finish cleaning yourself up?"

Firebird nodded, still studying the lighter in his hands.

"Cool, I'll see you out there then." She placed her hand to the back of his head, drew him toward her and kissed him on the forehead. "Oh, damn, are you bleeding?" She withdrew her hand and showed him the red, sticky blood on her fingers before she pulled his head forward and searched through his short-cropped hair for the source of the blood.

"No, I hit a guy in the nose with my head, it's his blood. Sorry about that." He gathered her hand and pulled wet wipes from a pack on the table. He gently wiped the blood from her fingers, and the palm of her hand before he gently kissed each cleaned finger. His hands were calloused and strong giving her an idea of the power behind his young body. His eyes locked on hers, she couldn't move, caught in his gaze like a gazelle to a lion.

Firebird stood, his arms circling gently around her beautiful body. He pulled her close, her breathing coming in sweet little pants as he lowered his head closer to hers. Ever so gently he brushed his lips across hers. Her sharp intake of breath came a moment before she opened to him, taking his lips hard against hers.

She felt the power of his kiss sing through her body, every nerve was alight, soaking in the sensations of him. His scent, his heat, his taste, his touch. She knew, she would never taste another man like him, he was addictive, in the worst possible way.

They broke the kiss reluctantly, Jenna hearing her name being called up onto stage, Tiffany's voice breaking their spell.

"Jenna, get your ass up here now or Dimitri's gonna pitch a fit." She looked at the two of them as she stopped at the curtain, eyes wide and mouth agape, she'd caught them out. "You two can play tonsil hockey later."

Chapter Eleven

Jenna's shift had finally finished. The bar was quiet and the die-hard drunken patrons were being ushered out. She waved at Firebird, smiling as she remembered the kiss they had shared in the dressing room. She watched as he pulled away before she got into her car and started it. Her mind was still on the handsome biker as she pulled out of the carpark. His eye had swollen a little bit, but it wasn't as bad as it could have been. She drove down the street a few blocks until she realised, she'd left her purse back at the club.

"Damnit," she muttered as she turned around and drove back. She was lucky Dimitri was just closing up when she got back.

"Hey, Dimitri, forgot my purse." She ran up to him.

"Yeah sure, go get it." He lit up a cigarette, deactivated the security system and waited for her. She returned a few minutes later, purse in hand.

"Thanks." As she walked past him, his hand shot out and grabbed her. He spun her around until her back was pressed hard against the brick wall.

"You need to stop leading on the hired help. You don't belong to him, you belong to my uncle." His voice was hard, threatening against her ear.

"Wh… what?" She was confused.

"The biker. Firebird. Don't fucking tease his cock like you tease mine, or you'll regret it." He leaned closer, his tongue darted out and licked her cheek. "Just remember, you have a contract with us, so no other strip club will take your sexy ass." He grinned, his hand reached around to grope and rub her through her jeans. "You and I could have some fun you know, I'm sure my uncle wouldn't mind a special video of just the two of us."

Jenna turned her head to the side and closed her eyes, trying to stop the fear from overcoming her. The stench of his breath mingled with cigarette smoke didn't help the churning of her stomach, nor did the heat of his body as he pressed himself against her.

"No?" Dimitri sighed. "Next time, perhaps. My uncle will be back here on Friday to see his favourite, pretty little slut." He pushed himself against her one more time before he released her.

She stumbled a little before dashing for her car, Dimitri's cruel laughter pierced the silence of the night.

Jenna's hand shook so hard she dropped her keys on the floor of her car. Hot tears trickled down her cheeks as she fumbled around for them. She finally got herself under control, and turned to see Dimitri still watching her. His cigarette burned red as he drew the noxious smoke into his lungs. His exhaled smoke rose to mingle with the pink fluorescent lighting which declared to the outside world there were *Live Nude Girls* inside.

He waved to her as she started her car and took off out of the parking lot. She didn't stop until she arrived home. She stumbled up the stairs to her small apartment and locked her door as soon as she stepped inside. Jenna leaned her back against the door, her body trembling as she thought back to what Dimitri had said to her.

Friday, Friday would herald another round of the hated VIP room. She slid down until her ass touched the threadbare carpet and she broke down.

Jenna knew one thing was for certain, she had to get away from her job. Away from Dimitri, Vladimir and Kasimir Rodchenko, her life might just depend on it, if not her sanity.

***

Tank leaned against the handlebars of his bike, watching the girls in the diner as they moved around. It had been almost a week since Firebird had trashed the strip club, doing battle with members of the Sons of Abaddon. His face had healed up, mostly.

"Fuck, I'd let her ride me…" he murmured softly as he gazed at the exposed legs of one of the girls.

"Dude, she's barely legal." Firebird scoffed before he took a bite out of his burger. "You wanna go inside for pounding some high schooler's pussy?" Firebird shook his head. "Wouldn't be worth it."

"That Jenna though, out of all the Class-A pussy at that club, man, she's top shelf." Tank leaned against the handlebars.

"Hands off her, brother." Firebird's voice was menacingly soft as he unwrapped more of his burger to devour. He wiped his stubble, smearing tomato ketchup over his chin, before he wiped again with the paper napkin, clearing the sticky sauce from his face

"You staking a claim, brother? Gonna get her to wear your *property of* patch?" Tank smirked as his eyes roved the ass of the girl he had targeted.

"Maybe. It's up to her. I've just gotta try and convince her it's a good idea." Firebird gobbled the last few bites of his burger and tossed the scraps to the birds. "Looks like our mark." He nodded to the beat up Chevrolet passing them, blue-grey smoke belching from the exhaust pipe.

"Hellooo, Hooper…" Tank grinned.

Hooper was one of the local drug dealers who bought in bulk from the MC. He had been late with payments and Firebird's father had tasked him and Tank to 'deal' with the problem.

The men kicked their bikes into life and followed the Chev. They kept their distance at least six cars behind so as not to alert their quarry with the beastly rumble of their bikes as they rode through the dark streets.

As they slowed in traffic at a set of lights, Firebird noticed Hooper put his arm around his female passenger's shoulders, and pull her head down into his lap. He shifted a little while he settled her into her 'job' before the lights changed.

"Someone's going for a happy ending." Firebird grinned.

"Lucky fucker."

"Yeah, well, his luck's going to run out very soon unless he's got the cash." Firebird put his bike back into gear as the lights changed and traffic started to move. They followed Hooper for a few miles until he pulled into the trailer park which was his home.

Tank and Firebird pulled up just inside the trailer park's entry. Hooper's shoddy trailer was in the middle of the trailer park. Bags of rubbish had been torn open by animals and week old pizza boxes were strewn across the yard. He helped the woman out of the car, having to push in on the passenger side door to get it to open.

"What a piece of shit. You know, you should go all 'Firebird Special' on that hunk of junk, brother." Tank grinned.

Firebird's lips curled and his throat worked as tried not to chuckle.

Their target entered his trailer, the woman in his arms giggling as he groped her. Firebird watched as he took the woman inside, the lights coming on in the trailer home.

"Let's give them a few minutes to enjoy their time together, then we'll go a-knocking." Firebird checked his watch. "Ten minutes."

Tank nodded and watched as the silhouettes came together in a lover's embrace beyond the yellow smoke-stained lace curtains covering the windows of Hooper's trailer.

"How's the eye?" Tank asked, breaking the silence after a few minutes.

"Fine, still a touch tender, but shit happens." Firebird shrugged.

"You mean the fucking Sons of Abaddon happened? Dude if I were there you'd be a lot prettier, and Jenna would be the one enjoying my charms."

"Fuck off asshole. Like I said, I'm staking a claim."

"Pussy-whipped," Tank muttered under his breath. "I never thought I'd see the day you got done Brother."

Firebird's response was to give Tank a hard shove against his shoulder. The big man didn't budge.

"Gotta try harder than that, piss-ant." Tank grinned.

Firebird shook his head, his smile visible in the dim light from the lonely streetlight that bathed the area in a dim glow.

Firebird gave the signal when they were at seven minutes. Tank rose, stretched his long legs and twisted his back to loosen his shoulders.

"Ready, Princess?" Firebird asked, "You sure you don't want to do some Yoga? Maybe Downward Facing Dog or Salute to the Sun?"

"Fuck you, asshole."

The two men moved swiftly from their hiding place to the door of the trailer. Firebird had a crowbar, his 'key', in hand in case the asshole didn't answer the door and it was locked. Firebird paused, his fist raised to knock on the aluminum door. His lips quirked up in a smirk as loud, erotic, moans, and the sounds of two bodies slapping against each other, skin on skin, came through the door.

"Sounds like someone's going to have their good times turn bad." Firebird grinned.

"Please daddy, can I bust the door down?" Tank's voice pleaded with a childish tone.

"Sure, go for it." Firebird handed Tank the crowbar.

Tank smirked with wicked purpose and kissed the curved head. "Baby, we are gonna have some fun tonight." He grinned devilishly in the dim light as the moans continued to rise to a caterwaul of passion. The big man slid the teeth of the crowbar between the door and doorjamb at the latch and thrust it downward. The metal screeched as it warped.

Firebird grabbed the edge of the door and pulled it open for Tank to enter, crowbar at the ready.

Tank burst in, a shout dying on his lips as he took in the scene before him. "Holy shit, Firebird, you gotta see this shit." Tank's voice bubbled with laughter.

"Mother fucker," Firebird stepped into the dimly lit trailer. Hooper was bent over the end of the dining booth of his trailer's kitchen, bare ass pointing to the roof, while his *girlfriend* was buried balls deep in Hooper's ass.

"Well, well, well, aren't we a dirty little fucker Hooper? Like to play with the lady boys do we?" Tank slid the hooked claw of the crowbar beneath Hooper's chin. The transvestite screamed and pulled free of his ass. Firebird pulled his pistol out and kept it aimed at the woman/man.

"Now, now, sweetheart, you sit down, we got a handle on this." Firebird tilted the gun indicating he wasn't asking. "And, put that away. Damn, I'll be having nightmares for a month of Sundays after seeing that shit." He grimaced when he noticed the erect cock the transvestite was sporting. Her… *his…?* dress bunched around it.

"Honey, your just jealous. You couldn't handle all of me, even if you tried. I'm too much for you bay-bee." The transvestite wiggled her head and pursed her overdone lips in a seductive air kiss.

"Yeah, yeah. You're delusional sweetheart."

Tank glanced from the naked man to the man/woman. "Hooper, you got balls, so does your girlfriend. I always thought you were a ladies man; never thought you'd go for a *lady-man*."

"Tank," Firebird kept his piece trained on the transvestite.

"Right, eight. So, Hooper, you owe our club some money, or are you spending it on breast implants on your girlfriend here? We know they aren't real. Nice work though."

Hooper's 'girlfriend' grabbed her fake tits and jiggled them at Tank, again, pursing her lips in a kissing motion. "You want to see how real they feel? I'm all yours, baby." She winked causing her fake eyelashes to bobble.

"Sweetheart, I'm not going there. I know what's between your legs *and* where it's been." Tank returned his attention to Hooper. "So you gonna pay up or what?"

"Yeah, yeah I got it." Hooper's voice was laced with nerves as his beady little rat eyes darted from left to right.

Tank allowed him up and watched as he moved toward a coffee tin. The dealer opened the lid and reached his hand in.

Tank didn't move fast enough. Hooper pulled a small handgun from the tin, spun around and shot Tank in the arm.

"Motherfucker!" Tank snarled and with lightning fast reflexes, he raised his good arm and staved in Hooper's head with the crowbar using more force than he intended. Time slowed to a crawl as the sickening crunch of bone sounded overly loud in the room. Blood and gray matter spattered the walls of the trailer as Hooper's head was broken open with the force of Tank's strike.

Hooper's eyes rolled up into the back of his head, he crumpled to the floor and convulsed as his damaged brain began to shut down.

The transvestite screamed, breaking the spell of time. Firebird's gunshot rang out, silencing their only witness.

"Fuck." Tank's eyes locked on the crowbar, the blood trickling down the iron bar to drip onto the scratched and worn linoleum floor.

"Yeah, Fuck." Firebird shook his head as he turned from the open eyes of the dead transvestite. "You all right, brother?" A red stain bloomed on Tank's arm.

"Yeah, should be, just hope none of the asshole's blood got near my wound, don't want no fucking AIDS from that fucker." Tank dropped the bar and it clattered to the floor.

"You going to be able to ride?" Firebird nodded to the gunshot wound.

"Yeah." Tank grabbed a grimy tea towel from the kitchen counter. He handed it to Firebird who tied it tightly against the bleeding wound.

"I should be okay, if not, I'll hit up Nurse Betty on the way." Tank referred to one of the nurses Firebird's father had banged in the past behind his mother's back and who they had kept on for emergency medical patch jobs.

"Get back to the compound, see if Dagger can get some prospect to come and help me clean up." Firebird e opened the door and let Tank out of the trailer.

"Will do," Tank said.

"Ride careful, brother." Firebird watched Tank walk into the darkness toward where they had stashed their bikes. He turned back to survey the damage he and

Tank had caused. He searched the trailer, finding a duffel bag filled with cash under the bed. They had gotten their payment, plus more, but lost one of their dealers. It wasn't going to be a big loss as Hooper was always late with his payments. The outcome, when Hooper had drawn a weapon on them was inevitable.

Firebird examined the trailer. His eyes were drawn to a napkin stuck to the fridge with a magnet. On it was written a phone number, and the name of the Sons of Abaddon's President. Times, dates and numbers with the street names of the drugs that the Sons of Abaddon peddled to their select drug dealers. It appeared Hooper had been two-timing with the Sons of Abaddon, and not hiding the evidence very well at all.

Firebird heard the roar of a Harley, echoed immediately by two others. He turned to peer through the window. Three members of the Abaddon boys had pulled up and were dismounting their bikes. Firebird watched a beat more as they started toward the trailer. He looked at the door that Tank had gone out not two minutes before.

Firebird was trapped.

"Fuck," he muttered.

Chapter Twelve

Jenna packed up the washing from the machine, One dryer had finally finished after chewing through ten dollars worth of quarters to get her load of washing dried properly, plus another seven for the washing machine. Laundry day was an expensive day and she still had one dryer running.

She wished she had her own washer and dryer, but her tiny little apartment had neither the space, nor laundry facilities, in the complex. She had no option but to go to the all night laundromat four blocks away, across from one of the dingiest trailer parks in town.

She had swept aside the brown paper bag occupying the plastic seat, flinching when the bottle inside smashed on the ground and the horrible stench of cheap whiskey permeated the air. She waited patiently while her washing dried in the machine, the colours swirling with each rotation.

Her mind drifted to Firebird, remembering the scent of his body as he pressed against her, the feel and taste of his lips against hers. She closed her eyes for a moment and wondered what it would be like to have him, to enjoy the sensation of him making love to her. She revelled in the pleasant fantasy until the high-pitched electronic beep of the dryer sounded, alerting her to the fact her laundry was finished.

She struggled with the large basket as she put the washing in her car.

Shouting in the trailer park drew her attention. A figure was struggling out of the window of one of the metal trailers. Fascinated, she watched as the man fell to the ground with a loud grunt. Two others burst from the trailer, bearing down on him. The figure looked up, struggling to his feet as the others grabbed him, and started to beat the hell out of the guy.

A third man left the trailer. Walking calmly, he called to the others. They dragged their captive to where the man stood in the dim light cast by the open door of the trailer. Jenna's heart almost stopped.

"Firebird."

She watched in horror as two men held him, and the third began to beat him mercilessly.

Blood spurted from his mouth as he took a right hook, then a left. His assailant bearing down on him with strike after strike. Jenna closed the door, jumped into her car, turned the key and started it up. She watched as the two men who held Firebird threw him to the ground. He landed on his hands and knees, head lowered, spitting blood.

She put the car into gear and drove slowly forward with her lights off until she had a better view. What she saw next made her heart skip a beat.

The guy who had been beating the shit out of Firebird reached behind him and pulled his gun. The other two goons stood a step or two behind him, watching as the attacker took aim. They seemed to be coming closer to her at speed, but the roar of her engine snapped Jenna out of her trance-like state. The first body hit her hood and smashed into her windscreen. Two other thumps alerted her that she had hit the other men at a glancing blow, their bodies rolled away from the car as she plowed through them.

She hit the brakes, her car skidding in the gravel road of the trailer park. She breathed hard while she collected her senses, and with shaking hands, put the car into park. Her passenger side door opened and she screamed.

"Jenna. It's me, Firebird." His voice broke through her hysterics.

"Oh my god! Oh my god! I hit them, I fucking hit them!" Her voice reached a hysterical pitch.

"It's okay, you need to drive. Get out of here." Firebird settled in her passenger seat. "Just drive baby, we'll sort this out later."

"But my car. My windscreen. Oh god, do you think they're okay?"

"Baby." Firebird swivelled in his seat and captured her face in his hands. "Listen to me, sweetheart. We need to get the fuck out of here. I'll fix your car, just get us out of here okay?"

Jenna nodded, rivers of tears cascaded down her face. She put the car into gear and took off out of the trailer park, past the injured and groaning men she had taken out.

"You saved my life tonight." Firebird used his undershirt to dab the blood oozing from his cut lip. He winced as he shifted, bruised ribs protesting the movement as his adrenalin returned to normal levels.

"Are, are you okay? Oh my god, he was going to kill you." Jenna was trying hard to process everything.

Firebird reached over, placing his hand over hers. "I'm okay, you did good. Get us somewhere safe and we'll talk, okay?"

Jenna nodded. "Okay." She spoke softly, the lights from the street illuminating her face, skin pale and streaked with mascara and tear tracks.

Firebird leaned over and gently kissed her cheek. "You did good, baby." He offered her assurance as he reached up and gently caressed her face.

She smiled wanly and nodded, sniffling a little through a fresh batch of tears. A smear of blood marred her cheek from his hand.

She pulled into her parking spot, turned off the ignition and remained where she was. In the driver's seat, stunned.

***

Firebird startled her with a gentle touch on her shoulder and she spun to face him.

"Is this your place?" he asked.

She nodded. "Okay, this is fine, I won't be here long, I promise." He climbed out of the car and hobbled around to her side, opening the door for her and helping her from the vehicle.

Jenna trembled so much, the keys slipped from her fingers. He let her pick them up, his body was screaming in pain, telling him he needed to heal again before he took on another round with the Sons of Abaddon.

The memory of having the gun pointed at his head was the clearest he'd ever known, then the confusion of the car rushing past, striking Feral and Kane before Dex was taken out. He had to hand it to Jenna, she was one brave chick.

He put an arm around her and guided her up the steps. "What number?"

"2D." Jenna pointed up another flight of stairs with a trembling hand, keys jangling. They headed up, she picked out her apartment key and after a few shaky attempts, she unlocked her door with Firebird's hand steadying hers. She flicked on the lights, illuminating her tiny living space and the two doors off to the side which led to the bathroom and her bedroom.

"Cosy." Firebird smiled and Jenna saw it was physically painful for him to attempt.

***

"Sit down, I'll get the first aid kit." Jenna flicked on the coffee maker as she walked past it toward the bathroom. As soon as she was through the door, everything in her stomach came up. She barely made it to the toilet before she threw up. Her stomach clenching with each retch. She coughed and spluttered, her hair cascading over her shoulders to get in the way of her vomit. She didn't care.

She moaned pitifully as strong hands pulled her hair out of the way, the vomit chunks sticking to some of the strands where they had been caught in their flight to the toilet bowl. Firebird knelt beside her, helping her through her nausea.

"Sorry, I should be patching you up, not throwing my guts up." She shivered with shock.

"You just went through some heavy shit, it's natural to be like this." Firebird tucked her hair behind her ears and caressed her face.

"Let's get us both cleaned up. I hope you don't mind, but I needed to use your phone, I'm still on the call, and I'll be right back. You clean yourself up, have a shower, and come out when you're ready, okay?" He smiled softly

"Okay." Jenna looked at herself in the mirror. She looked horrendous yet Firebird hadn't run for the hills decrying her shocking appearance.

She stripped off her clothing, running the water in the shower while Firebird returned to the living space to finish his call.

Chapter Thirteen

"…Yeah, I know, the bastard had a gun pointed to my head, Dagger. He was about to shoot me, then she comes in with her car, and fucking bam, bam, bam, she takes out all three of them."

Dagger spoke again.

Firebird heard the shower start running and stepped around the doorway, the bathroom door was ajar. He watched as her beautiful body entered the spray.

Dagger's words barely registered, something about her car and his bike.

Despite the pain his body was in, it responded to seeing Jenna nude. Sure he'd seen her tits and much of her ass before but that was on stage where she worked. Here, he didn't have to share her with a dozen drunk, horny old guys. Here, she was *his*.

He lowered his eyes and shook his head clear. "Yeah, her car's a mess. Front end damage, windscreen's fucked. I think I saw blood on the front fender. I know I've left a bit on the passenger side seat." He glanced up, watching as she soaped her body. "It was definitely Abaddon. The napkin has names, numbers, prices, money owed and the amount they had for him to deal. They didn't get it, I have it in my pocket. I think they were coming to check up on Hooper, maybe shake him for cash like we were. Now we know why he wasn't paying us for our deliveries, fucker was paying them."

His hard-on grew when Jenna arched her back and washed her hair. Her perfect breasts pushed outward as she reached back, gathering the wet tresses, scrubbing it clean. She stopped when she noticed him watching her and slowly drew her hand down between her breasts.

Distracted, Firebird only half-heard what Dagger was saying over the phone. "Yeah, I'll get back as soon as I can. Can you get one of the prospects to get my bike from the trailer park back to the clubhouse? I'll get someone to pick me up as soon as I'm done here." Firebird ended the call without listening to Dagger's reply.

He pulled his cut from his shoulders, wincing as his ribs protested the motion. His eyes locked on Jenna and she watched him move closer. Her need deep within her soulful eyes. Firebird shed his clothing with each step until he stood before her, naked. His tattoos etched in a mixture of dark and vibrant colours over the lay of his muscular body. Her eyes roved over him, taking in each curve of muscle under skin.

Her body called out to him to touch her. His hand raised a little, a non-threatening gesture before he looked to her for permission to touch her body. Jenna smiled, her hand guiding his to where she needed his touch. The scent of her soap enticed him closer, his sweat and blood-splattered body washing clean in the hot water.

Jenna soaped his skin, taking care over his painful ribs and damaged skin from his beating. Her touch was gentle, but sizzling in the sensations he felt at her touch. He moaned softly as her hand tentatively reached down to his cock, the soap sliding and lathering up as she worked him.

He placed his hands to either side of her head, her back against the cracked tiles in the shower as she gained confidence and her hands worked him hard into a frenzy. He felt himself coming closer to that dangerous edge, an edge which he would fall off in sweet ecstasy at her hands. His breathing hitched as he grabbed her hand. Jenna looked up at him, he smiled. The seduction game would continue, but now, it was his turn.

He leaned forward, his lips tracing butterfly kisses across her jawline before he moved to claim her lips, her soft moans telling him he was on the right track as she shifted, pressing her wet body against his. Her hands guided his to her breasts where expert fingers plucked and softly pinched at her budding nipples until they reached tight peaks.

She gasped against his lips, he took the opportunity to introduce his tongue to hers, and they danced passionately while his hands made busy work, trailing down to the apex of her thighs where she opened her legs for him to explore.

Firebird didn't need to be asked twice. She moaned again, as his fingers found their way between her folds, up to the hard little nub of her clit. Her gasp told him she was definitely enjoying his explorations as much as he was.

"Don't fuck me…" she whispered.

"What?" Firebird was taken aback at her request.

"Make love to me, don't just fuck me." Jenna panted.

"Whatever you want, baby." Firebird returned his mouth to hers in a sweet, passionate kiss. "Anything for you, Jenna." She trembled under his fingers as he shifted himself between her legs. His hard cock pressing against the warm lips of her pussy he slid in, hearing her gasp as she took his throbbing cock inside her.

Firebird gently took her ass in his hands, letting her ride him at her own pace while he pressed worshipful kisses against her body. He encouraged her movements a little with small thrusts which quickly became deeper and harder, Jenna's body taking him deep as she moaned, wrapping her legs and arms around his body. Firebird had never felt anything like the heavenly body he was deeply embedded in, and was wrapped tightly around him as she clenched herself around his cock.

Her gasps sounded harsh but blissful in his ears with each thrust of his hips, hitting her in just the right place so that her moans were musical and delightful for him to hear. He leaned his head down and lifted one of her breasts into his mouth, suckling the nipple.

Jenna's orgasm exploded through her body, her cunt tightening around him as he moved inside her. He moaned with a mouthful of her breast, his own release coming on fast and hard as he speared her, pressing her against the tiles. Their bodies spent, exhausted and aching for different reasons.

"Fuck, Jenna," he whispered. "If I never get to be with you again, I'll be a very happy man." His mind was addled by the post orgasmic bliss.

Firebird gently let her down, reluctant to be removing himself from her body, but knowing it was necessary. He washed himself off as the water went from just barely warm to ice cold, letting Jenna get out of the shower to dry herself off and get dressed.

She passed him a towel when he turned the water off, she was shy around him again. He watched as she wrapped a dressing gown around her body and scurried out of the bathroom without another word.

Firebird dried himself off, locating his underwear and blood-splattered jeans. He knew his t-shirt and cut were in the same state, but he had no other clothes. Jenna was pouring coffee for them both when a knock at the door startled her, she spilled the coffee over her hand.

"Damn it." She thrust her hand under cold water.

"I'll get that." Firebird reached for his piece sitting on the kitchen table.

Jenna's eyes widened when she saw it in his hands.

"It's okay, it's probably one of my brothers come to pick me up."

Jenna nodded and kept her hand under the water, while Firebird went to the door. He opened it slowly, peeking through the crack. Dagger stood with his arms crossed and not looking too pleased.

"You must really like to fuck things up boy-o. Just wait till your old man hears about this one." He grinned, then frowned, sniffing the air. "Do I smell sex on you?" he asked with a devilish grin, his eyes flicking to Jenna as she patted dry the small scald on her hand.

"Blood, piss and a little bit of brain matter." Firebird said, looking over his clothes.

"Actually, it's Colombian Blend." Jenna interjected, bringing two cups over to the men.

Dagger tilted his head back and laughed, accepting the cup.

Jenna cast a quick glance to Firebird, their eyes met and her heart beat a little faster. Firebird noticed how her hands shook as she poured herself another cup of coffee. He hoped she would be okay once he left with Dagger.

Chapter Fourteen

Jenna looked at the other girl sitting on the bed. She wore a red lacy bra and G-string set, leaving little to nothing to the imagination. Her own outfit mirrored the stranger's, but was jet black. She stood as far away from the bed as she could, without bumping into Mr. Rodchenko, who watched her like a hawk might watch a mouse.

Vladimir looked through the eyepieces of each camera. "The setting is good, but I think, we might have you in Daniella's place, Jenna. He smiled, and pulled a pair of black velvet ropes from his pocket. Dimitri came into the VIP room, and perused the scene.

"Looks good. Ready when you are, Uncle." He nodded to his uncle who was stripping down to his underclothes.

"Yes, it will be a very good movie. We are getting interest from new investors who are keen to try out their acting skills with our girls." He reached out and grabbed a handful of Jenna's left ass cheek. She squeaked in surprise.

"Particularly with our Jenna here, but I think I'll keep her for my own personal films." He pushed her roughly toward the bed. Vladimir tossed the ropes to the brunette woman who seemed to have no problem with what they were doing, and she tied Jenna's hands to the bar that formed part of the bedhead.

"Now, get comfortable, and spread those legs." Dimitri checked the ties. They were tight against her skin and she couldn't help but whimper in fear. She was never a fan of the tie up games her ex-boyfriend would get her to play in the bedroom, and this situation made it much worse.

"Daniella, you may begin." Vladimir said to the other woman, she nodded and started to crawl back onto the bed "Roll camera!"

Jenna watched as the woman began to lick slowly up her leg, her perfectly manicured hands holding Jenna's trembling limbs as she moved up from her calf to her thigh, pushing her at the knee until her leg bent, opening her up a little more. Jenna's breathing hitched when Daniella's fingers slid up under the inner hem of her G-string, and the tip of her nail gently touched the edge of her pussy.

"Relax and enjoy, sweetheart." She purred. "We are all going to have some fun." She smiled.

Rodchenko handed Daniella a pair of scissors and she cut away the G-string, pulling the small triangle of material down, exposing Jenna's pussy.

Jenna watched as the woman licked her lips and leaned down, her mouth pressing a soft kiss against Jenna's nether lips

Behind them, Rodchenko watched, his cock already in his stroking hands.

"Good, good." He crooned. "Lick her harder, eat that sweet pussy, Daniella." He ordered and the movements of Daniella's tongue intensified, pushing harder against Jenna's pussy, sliding between her lips to the centre.

Jenna squirmed, trying to move away from the intrusive tongue of the woman between her legs, but she was unable to move, bound as she was to the bed.

The camera moved closer to where the action was. Daniella pressed down on Jenna's thighs while she raised her ass for Rodchenko to mount. He grunted behind her as he thrust his cock deep inside Daniella's pussy, her moans vibrated through Jenna's core.

At that very moment, Jenna hated everyone in that room, everyone who had brought her to this situation, including herself. Hot, angry tears rolled down her face as she wept silently. Daniella's tongue worked against her clit.

"Come on, Jenna. For fuck's sake, at least fake it." Dimitri growled as he shifted the camera angle slightly to take in more of the action behind Daniella. Jenna closed her eyes and grit her teeth, willing this ordeal to be over so she could get home, where her fate awaited. She was so tired of being used and abused. The only one who seemed to care about her was Firebird, and she was far too ashamed of everything she was going through to confide in him.

She had already decided. It would all end tonight.

***

Firebird watched as the girls danced around the poles, the customers wolf-whistling and waving notes to entice them to come closer kept his attention. He didn't notice Jenna making her way out of the club.

He watched the girls working, but when it was Jenna's turn, Amber took the stage. Firebird frowned, knowing that Jenna usually didn't miss a shift. He turned to Charlie and raised an eyebrow in question. Charlie shrugged his shoulders as he wiped dry a beer glass behind the bar.

Hannah swanned by, her jet black hair and striking blue teddy tight against her curves.

"Hannah, you seen Jenna? Isn't she supposed to be up on stage?" He stopped her gently by grasping her upper arm.

"She went home. She said she wasn't feeling well, though she looked fine to me." Hannah pulled her arm from Firebird's grip.

"Okay, thanks," he said as she walked away from him.

He frowned, this wasn't like Jenna. He waited until the end of his shift. Thankfully, it was uneventful. Firebird strode with purpose to his bike, something was bugging him about Jenna's sudden sickness, and he couldn't quite put his finger on it.

He started his Harley and pulled out of the parking lot, the echoing growl of his engine reverberating around the walls of the strip club. He felt the powerful engine driving the Harley through the streets, an extension of his body as he rode toward the woman who was quickly becoming a starring feature in his mind when he jacked off at night.

Her car had been repaired in the past week by Dagger and two of the prospects at the mechanic's shop that the club owned and he had returned it to her. Jenna had been so happy, running her hands over the paintwork. It was as good as new, and was running much better than it had before. It now sat in its parking space outside her apartment building.

He pulled up beside her car and checked the hood, it wasn't very warm, but showed him she had been home for at least an hour or so. He took the steps two at a time, the leather of his boots creaking with each heavy step on the crumbling concrete stairs. Her door loomed. The small window beside the door showed her TV was on, the blue light of a late-night infomercial flickering against the lace curtains. He knocked on the door, his fist pounding hard against the cheap plywood.

"Jenna? It's Firebird."

There was no answer, he tried again, pounding on the door a little harder. Still no answer. By the fourth time he shouted out to her to answer the door, the next-door-neighbour opened her door. Her hair in curlers and a threadbare-looking bathrobe and filthy bunny slippers completed the look of a disgruntled housewife. She puffed on a cigarette

"You gonna quit pounding on that door and hollerin' or am I gonna call the cops?"

Firebird glared at her and turned his attention to the window. Peering through the lace curtains, he saw Jenna's arm hanging over the couch. His eyes were drawn to the floor, where a medicine bottle lay on its side.

"Do you know if she takes any medication?" he asked the neighbour.

"No, but she asked if I had any sleeping pills she could borrow tonight." The woman said, crossing her arms and taking another drag on her cigarette.

"Sleeping pills?" Firebird glanced from the window to the neighbour. "Did you give her any?"

"Yeah, a whole bottle of them, I don't have no use for them anymore, they don't work on me."

Firebird didn't listen to anything else she had to say, he turned his shoulder against the front door and rammed against it. The door thumped in its frame as he continually threw his shoulder against it until it burst open, the deadlock falling to the floor as he broke it away from the cheap door.

He raced to Jenna's side and found a puddle of vomit on the sofa dripping from her lips to the floor.

"Fuck."

"You gonna pay for that door?" the neighbour asked.

"Get a fucking ambulance here now, she's overdosed!"

"Fucking junkies. She'd be better off dead."

Firebird scowled at her. "They were your pills, bitch. You're just as responsible, now call a fucking ambulance!" He shouted at the woman before he turned to check on Jenna. She was breathing but her breaths were shallow and slow, barely there. Her heart rate was slow, sluggish.

Firebird called her name and slapped her lightly on the face to try to rouse her. She didn't move, nor did she make a sound as he rolled her onto her side and pressed two fingers between her lips, clearing her mouth of vomit. Sitting and pulling her onto his lap, he held her close, rocking her, praying for her to live.

"Hold on, Baby." He barely heard the woman on the phone to the emergency services, all his attention was on Jenna's unconscious form.

"Come on, stay with me, baby." He begged her as tears of fear broke free and ran down his stubbled cheeks to drip into her paling face.

Chapter Fifteen

The constant *beep-beep-beep* of the alarm roused her. She moaned, reaching over to slap it, hoping to snag the large snooze button and kill the incessant noise. A large hand grabbed hers, the fingers stroking over her palm. Jenna's eyes shot open and she looked around, confused as to where she had woken up.

The sterile cream and light green-blue walls of the hospital ward greeted her and awareness broke through the haze of whatever she had still in her system.

The pressing sensation and the soft hiss of oxygen as it pushed through the plastic mask on her face made her feel claustrophobic, she reached up with her free hand to push the offending mask away. The hand that held hers moved, pushed away the hand seeking to free her of the mask.

"No, leave it there, baby." A familiar male voice soothed. "You need to leave it there. Everything is going to be okay." He reached up and brushed hair away from her forehead. Her vision was a touch blurry but she looked over to see the worried face of Firebird. Brett.

Hot, angry tears fell from her eyes as she remembered what she had done. She was ready to end it after the last VIP session with Rodchenko and his cronies.

She had been determined never to wake up from the sleeping pills she had taken from Mrs. Torres in the apartment next door. She felt alone, pathetic, and burdensome. She never wanted her family to discover what the Russians were making her do, let alone Brett.

She closed her eyes and wept. His hands stroked her cheeks, catching each tear as they fell and wiping them away. His voice soothed her shattered spirit. His warm lips pressed against her temple and she reached up, putting her hand around his head and holding him against her. Desperate for some human contact that wasn't degrading or destructive to her body and soul.

Firebird slid his arms around her, pulling her up slightly from the bed and into his arms. She felt the pull of the IV in her hand. The sting of the needle as it shifted slightly and the coolness of the IV fluids as they ran into her hand and up her arm. She shuddered as she sobbed against his shoulder. His hands stroked the bareness of her back through the opening in her hospital gown. His touch was warm and comforting, bringing a splash of colour into her grey, and lifeless world. A nurse entered the ward and looked over her charts.

"Well, good morning Miss." The nurse checked the monitor and IV lines.

Firebird lowered Jenna back on the bed, easing her up against the pillows while the nurse adjusted the bed to a sitting position.

"You gave your boyfriend quite a scare there. You're one lucky young woman to have a man who cares so much about you." She smiled, her eyes flicking to Firebird. "I think some of your friends are out in the waiting room looking for you. You might need to go out there and see them, sir."

"Yeah, I'll be back in a minute." He kissed Jenna lightly.

"She'll be okay. The doctor will be in soon to speak with her." The nurse assured him.

Firebird nodded before leaving Jenna alone with the nurse.

"He wouldn't leave your side," the nurse said as she checked the IV in her hand. "We almost had to get Security to remove him, but he calmed down once we told him you had a strong heartbeat. He's a cutie too. I'd keep him if I were you." The nurse patted her on the hand and left her bedside.

Jenna sighed, her thoughts drifting to Firebird, and what the nurse had told her. He cared for her, so much he had come to her. She wondered if she deserved him. The dark thoughts in her mind coiled like a snake, ready to strike at the spark of life she held within her heart.

***

Firebird stalked down the hallway. His father, Dagger and Tank stood up. They had been waiting for him. His father put an arm around his shoulders and guided him over to a small couch.

"Son. What's going on with you? Is this thing serious with this girl?"

"I'm hoping it will be. I feel things for her that I've never experienced before."

His father sighed and shook his head. "It's hormones, son, this will pass."

"I don't think so, Dad. This shit, it's real, y'know? I feel alone when she's not near me, I get jealous of other men touching her, looking at her."

"She's a damned stripper, son, and she belongs to the Russians. She's got a contract with them. You're not to touch her. Kasimir Rodchenko has a mark on her. She belongs to him." He saw his son's face fall.

"What, the Russian mob boss? She's his?" the surprise on Firebird's face was total.

"You didn't know?" His father shook his head. "Put her out of your mind, son. She's not for you." His father placed his hand on his shoulder. "I need your head in the game son, we've got bigger problems than you pining over untouchable pussy. The Sons of Abaddon are muscling in on our turf. Dagger did some digging and found out a few more of our dealers have taken on the Abaddon's side."

Firebird looked at his father, Dozer appeared to be exhausted. The Club had greyed his hair and brought more lines to his face than a lifetime of riding would have brought to any man's face. But it was a lifetime of riding through the storm that was the life of an MC member. Through blood, loyalty, stints in prison, fights with friends, family and foes, his father had borne it. It was obvious on his face, he was true to his club. The club was family. More than family. It was his life.

Firebird wondered for the first time in his own life, if he was truly cut out for the life. He looked up into his father's eyes and saw pride, hope and fear.

"You can count on me, Dad." He glanced down the hallway to Jenna's room. He wanted to go to her, to let her know he had to go, and to tell her he would be back, but he knew he couldn't. Not with his father watching, and not with what he had been told about his beautiful, broken girl.

"Good, come on, Red needs a lift home, she was visiting her mother here, she's waiting by your bike.

"Yeah I'll give her a ride. Just gotta call someone to come and get Jenna." He still felt responsible for her.

"All right, just be quick." His father indicated the payphone nearby.

***

Jenna watched the doctor as he went over her charts. "You're very lucky to be alive, young lady. However, I'm afraid I have some bad news, you've lost your baby."

"M…my baby?" Jenna put her hands over her stomach. "I was pregnant?"

"Yes, you were. I'm sorry, but you miscarried as a result of your overdose." The doctor signed off on the chart, his eyes scornful. "A counsellor will be visiting shortly. You need to get yourself together, young lady. You have a lot to live for." He turned to leave, but she snagged the back of his white coat.

"Doctor, how far along was I?"

"About five weeks along."

"But I was on the pill!"

"Did you take any antibiotics during that time? They will negate the effects of the contraceptive pill."

"I had a virus about six weeks ago." She remembered taking a course of antibiotics during that time. The child had to have been Rodchenko's. She shuddered in revulsion, thinking he had impregnated her.

The doctor left and she rolled over, ignoring the world around her. She wanted to be in Firebird's arms right now, but he hadn't returned to her room.

An hour later, he still wasn't back. Tiffany arrived with a bunch of flowers.

"Was firebird out there?" she asked as Tiff set the flowers into a glass vase.

"He called me to come check on you. I thought I passed him on the way here." She sat on the chair by Jenna's bed. She appeared uncomfortable.

"What is it, Tiff?" Jenna prodded.

"He was out with some of the other guys from his club." She paused. "There was some red-headed chick on the back of his bike."

Jenna frowned, unsure of what to make of the information. Maybe Tiff was mistaken.

"Look, sweetie, don't worry about him, okay? The doctor says you can leave tomorrow; they just want to make sure you're okay. Then you're going to crash at my place for a while until you're back on your feet." Tiff took her hand and squeezed it reassuringly.

Chapter Sixteen

"So, here we are," Tiff opened the door to her apartment.

"Thanks again, Tiff." She set down the bag she had packed. Her apartment had been ransacked in her absence, the door hadn't been fixed while she was in hospital. Almost all of her valuables and money had been stolen.

It was a major setback in her plans. Her college fees for the semester were due and her rent had a large fee tacked on for the cost of the locksmith who had come too late to fix her locks and save her possessions.

Tiff had come to her rescue once she broke the rental agreement at her apartment, offering her spare bedroom to Jenna.

"I have the spare room set up for you, rent is due every Friday, utilities we'll deal with later, let's just get you settled in." She wrapped her arms around Jenna in a tight bear hug. "Things will be better soon, sweetheart."

"I hope so." Jenna's thoughts drifted to Firebird. He hadn't called or come to see her again, and her mind played on what Tiff had said about him with some red-headed chick on the back of his bike. She followed Tiff around like a ghost while she showed her around the small apartment that was to be her home until she was back on her feet again.

***

Jenna had a few days off work to recover, and she spent them watching terrible daytime television. A knock at the door roused her from a bored half-slumber while some over enthusiastic television presenter tried to sell some fantastic new product that would save time, money and drive you insane with the crappiness of the product. She pushed the blanket off her lap and padded barefoot to the door, unlatching the bolt and chain as she opened it.

Kasimir Rodchenko stood with a leering smile on his face. Behind him stood two men in leather cuts, facing away from the door. *Sons of Abaddon MC* was emblazoned on the black leather in a white curved rocker. A skull with flames burned in the empty eye sockets. Below it sat three smaller skulls, each grinning with nefarious intent and with matching flames in their own, smaller eye sockets.

"Ahh, Jenna. It's good to see you have recovered. My friends here, have expressed an interest in engaging in your special *services*."

She shook her head but Rodchenko laughed. Jenna threw the door back in his face, only to have it pushed back against her. She stumbled backward, her heel catching on the rug covering the worn floorboards. She grunted as she fell, hitting her head on the floor and seeing stars flash in her eyes.

"Ahh, now, now, my pretty girl, you're mine to do with as I please, and it pleases me to have you filmed with these young men here, who have done right by me and my organisation." He crouched down by her as the two bikers entered the apartment. She whimpered in fear as the men gripped her arms and hauled her up.

Rodchenko smiled darkly as he reached up and caressed her face. "This is going to be a beautiful movie, my sweet. You are my star." He pushed his lips against her possessively. She struggled futilely in the grip of the two bikers who held her. The men walked her out of the apartment. Rodchenko closed the door behind him.

Jenna was dragged to a black town car, behind it, four bikers sat waiting with their bikes idling. Rodchenko slid into the back seat, while the two bikers pushed her in beside him and closed the door. The roar of their bikes behind them reverberated through the car.

Hot tears trickled down Jenna's cheeks. Rodchenko put his hand on her bare leg, shifting his hand up to the shorts she wore. "You're going to look so beautiful. I know you have a thing for bikers, so you'll enjoy this." He squeezed her thigh.

Jenna lowered her head, and peered through the side window as the world passed her by. Her body trembled in fear as she was taken to the club where her fate awaited.

***

Firebird killed the rumbling engine. For the past few days he'd tried to put Jenna out of his mind. He'd just returned from a job with Dagger and was exhausted. He flopped down on his bed and looked up at the posters of naked chicks he had stuck on his ceiling. Their faces morphed into Jenna's. Their bodies changed to her perfect curves as he studied the images.

Something felt wrong, Jenna's eyes bore into him, fear-filled. He knew there was something happening to her, something bad. Why else would she try to kill herself?

"Firebird… help me…" her voice whispered in his mind. He woke with a jolt. Had he been dreaming? The pictures on the ceiling had returned to their buxom original forms, the pouting lips of the closest model teasing him as her hands were frozen in the image of her plucking her hard nipple with one hand while her other rested between the lips of her pussy.

Firebird rose, working his head from side-to-side and getting the kinks out. A knock at his door had him on his feet and opening the door to find Dagger grinning at him. "Hey brother, you got some hours to kill at the strip club? Dimitri wants a few extra hands tonight, supposed to have a few college students in, extra cash in your back pocket."

Firebird nodded. "Yeah, I'll be down in a sec."

"Ride out with Tank, he's taking his truck, his bike's got a flat tire, picked up a nail on the road earlier tonight."

"Ouch." Firebird winced in sympathy as he pulled on his cut.

"Yeah. I'll let him know to wait for you. Hurry up and make yourself all pretty, princess."

Firebird flipped him the bird.

Dagger laughed as he turned away and headed back to the common room. Firebird finished getting his gear together, grabbed his bike keys and slipped them into his pocket. His two pieces slid easily into the holsters, one at his ankle, the other at the small of his back, fitting snug between the waistband of his jeans. He cast his eyes around his room one last time, checking to make sure he'd left nothing behind before he headed downstairs

Tank sat at the bar, flirting with the blonde barmaid who giggled at his attempts to woo her into his bed for a night of – in his words - 'passionate and raw animalistic sex'.

Firebird slapped him on the shoulder. "Won't last that long, five minutes tops." Firebird held his hand up, five fingers on one hand splayed to prove his point.

"Asshole." Tank shoved him as he got up.

"Come on, stud, let's get going." Firebird headed for the door.

Chapter Seventeen

Jenna awoke, her arms were numb as she swung from the chains holding her. A bright, almost blinding light shone down on her. Her bare feet barely touched the plush carpeted floor below her. Her back stung from the whip they had used on her. She moaned at the pounding pain racing through her head.

"Ahh, the princess is awake." A gruff voice came from the darkness

"Water… please…" she begged, her voice barely more than a rasp in her dry throat.

"Water? We'll see. I think she might be ready for the next round." The voice suggested.

"No… please, let me go…"

A hand reached out from the darkness and gripped her chin painfully. "*We'll* tell you when *we're* done, then we'll give some copies of these tapes to Firebird, show him what it means to fuck with the Sons of Abaddon." The hand dropped from her chin to roughly grope at her breasts.

She cried out as the man gripped her right breast in a cruel grip, while another man moved behind her, pushing her legs apart. She screamed, struggling helplessly as the man forced himself on her.

***

In between breaks of the men taking her, she listened to them talk with Rodchenko, who watched from the Queen Anne chair. Smoking a Cuban cigar and enjoying top-shelf whiskey.

"Yes, yes. So the distribution of my weapons and drugs will be taken over by you, just kill the Maelstrom dogs who run the trucks and the security on my shipments. I'll leave the details up to you. It will be most profitable for all involved, I think." Rodchenko pulled on the cigar and blew the smoke in rings that danced lazily in the subdued light.

Jenna's body jerked with the rough thrusts of the biker behind her. Blood trickled down her arms from small cuts made by the cuffs around her wrists. Her body ached. Her most intimate places burned with the abuse, and all the while her position and body was reflected in the glass of the lens of a camera.

She could feel her eye and lower lip swelling up from the beating she had taken. The haze of exhaustion blurred her vision as the biker behind her finished with a strangled, impassioned grunt. She fell gratefully into the darkness that beckoned her.

***

Firebird nodded to the prospects who worked the door. The club was busy. Dimitri smiled a welcome to the boys as they walked through the crowd. Tiffany and another two girls worked the poles while others swanned about, enticing men to part with their cash for a lap dance in the back rooms.

"Ah, glad you could come boys. We have some VIPs in tonight. Friends of my uncle are up in the VIP room."

"Where do you want us?" Tank asked, as Firebird scanned the room for Jenna, something niggled at the back of his mind.

"Main floor, just keep an eye out for drunken idiots.

"Jenna on tonight?" Firebird asked, looking around the club, but unable to see her. His gut instinct burned with the sense she was nearby.

"She's here, but she's entertaining in the VIP room." Dimitri said with a knowing smile that seemed to rub Firebird the wrong way. Dimitri turned and walked off, heading to the back office.

"What's up, brother?" Tank asked.

"Not sure, but I got a bad, bad feeling, brother." He looked around. "Jenna is supposed to be off for a few days. She's supposed to be recovering from her visit to the hospital. Why would she be here tonight?"

"No idea man, maybe they needed more pussy on the floor, busy as it is tonight." Tank settled in to watch the floor.

Firebird bristled beside Tank. "Going for a walk, man."

"All right, brother." Tank nodded, casting his eyes out to the main floor, searching for signs of trouble.

Firebird walked through the crowd of drunken, leering men as they ogled the girls working the poles. Charlie nodded to Firebird as he approached the bar.

"Hey! Good to see you, how's things?" He poured Firebird a beer and slid it to him. He guzzled the brew and put the glass down on the bar

"That bad huh?" Charlie took the empty glass. "Tiff said you found our Jenna. I'm glad you got to her in time." He sighed, picking up a bar rag and a beer glass that had just come from the washer under the bar. "She's a worry that girl. She's always up in the VIP area. She's got a smile plastered on her face when she goes in, but there's no life in her when she walks out, and even though she's got that smile on her face, it's just for show. That girl is dying inside. She needs something to bring her back." Charlie leaned forward, pointing the rag he'd used to dry the glass in Firebird's direction

"I've never seen her happier than when she's spent time with you." He looked meaningfully at Firebird. "She needs you." He put the glass away and picked up another, drying it vigorously. He didn't meet Firebird's gaze as he put the dried glass with its brothers in the rack. "And I think you need her too."

Firebird nodded. She was constantly in his thoughts, even though his father had forbidden him from seeing her. He had been a good son, a good Maelstrom brother and had stayed away, even though it tore him apart inside.

He couldn't do it anymore. "She's in VIP you said?" Firebird glanced up to the mirrored window that he knew led into the VIP room.

"Yeah. Should be done soon, but they've been in there for hours. Some guys with leather jackets like yours, but the thing on the back is different, not a tornado over a bike engine, but like four skulls."

"Four skulls?" Firebird turned to face Charlie, instantly alert.

"Yeah, four skulls, one bigger than the others, formed like this." He pulled three shot glasses out and arranged them in a line under his dirty beer glass.

"Fuck." *Sons of Abaddon*. "Thanks." He pushed away from the bar and headed through the pounding music of the strip club.

"Hey honey, want a private dance?" The sultry voice of one of the new girls reached his ears as soft fingers trailed down his arm, stopping his progress towards the VIP area.

"Sorry babe, I'm working here."

"Maybe next time, when I'm not working." She purred.

"Stephanie, get your cute ass over here. girl. Leave Firebird alone." Tiff called the new girl over, waving her to a group of young men who were flashing wads of cash, and enticing the girls to play.

Firebird moved on, heading toward the unguarded staircase leading to the VIP room. He took the stairs two at a time, his heart pounding in his chest as he ascended to the second floor. The beat of the music moved closer to the VIP door. There was no-one on the door working security, just as there was no-one working the entry to the VIP stairs.

He put his hand on the doorknob, his hand wrapping around the fake gold of the ornate handle. The door opened with his push. The world stopped as he looked upon Jenna's bruised and fearful face, jostling with the savage thrusts of one of the Sons of Abaddon as he took her from behind.

"Firebird…" she gasped as she recognised him. *"Help me…"*

Chapter Eighteen

Firebird moved swiftly, a gun in his hand as the men around him moved to take him down. The door closed behind him, the gunfire deafeningly loud in the soundproofed room. Flashes from the gun illuminated his face as he took aim at each looming figure that came at him in the darkness.

The stench of gunpowder was acrid in his nostrils, as disgusting as the stench of the room, blood, sex and an underlying aroma of terror. The silence after his gun lowered was thick. Jenna's pained and heavy sobs broke through and he stepped over the bodies to reach her.

Her body was wracked with heavy sobs as he gathered her in his arms.

"Okay, baby, I've got you now. You'll be okay." He held her tight as she trembled against him. Blood from her wounds trickled over him. "Jenna, honey I need to find the key, so I can get you down from here and out of this hole."

She worked her mouth, her voice a pained whisper "Rodchenko, he has it." The pitiful sound of her voice broke his heart.

"Where is he, was he here?"

She nodded. "But he left a half hour ago, said something about business with their president." Her voice was barely above a choked whisper.

"Fuck." He kept a hand on her to let her know he was still with her, while he bent to pick up his piece. "Close your eyes, I'm going to shoot the chain on your cuffs and we'll get you out of here, okay?"

He studied her tortured eyes. He felt her tremble in fear as he held her naked and abused body against the warmth of his body. He raised the gun above his head, pressing the muzzle against the chains. "Okay, hold still sweetheart, this is going to be loud. He pressed her head against his chest, blocking her ear against the warmth of his shirt. He held a hand over her other ear, supporting her under the arm with his own. "One, two, three…" He fired the gun on three.

The chain broke cleanly. Jenna dropped toward the floor, her legs unable to hold her weight after her ordeal.

"I got you, baby. I got you." He dropped his gun and caught her as she fell.

"I'm gonna put you on the bed for a minute, okay? I need you to sit tight, and I'll be right back." He swept her up into his arms

"No, you'll leave me again." She sobbed, her hand clutching at his shirt, her blood smearing on the white material of his tee shirt.

"No baby, I promise I won't leave you, ever again." He held her tight against him as he lowered her onto the bed, ignoring the bodies of the Sons of Abaddon members he'd killed. He looked down at her, her face was swollen, one eye almost shut, her lip split and seeping blood. He didn't even want to know what damage the bastards had done to her internally.

"I *will* be back sweetheart, I just have to get Tank to help me get you away from here, okay?" He caressed her bruised face, trying to be gentle, knowing it must hurt like hell. He wrapped her in the coverlet on the bed, holding her tight against him.

"Please, don't leave me." Her whispered plea tore at his heart.

"I promise I'll be back." He pulled away reluctantly, leaving her in the covers, huddled in the foetal position on the bed. The stench of death and gunpowder surrounding them.

Firebird rushed from the VIP room and bolted down the stairs in search of Tank. He found him flirting with Tiffany while she collected a drinks order for her table.

"Brother, I need your help." His tone was urgent, his breath harsh in his lungs.

Tank stepped away from Tiff to look his brother over. "What is it, Firebird?" His eyes widened in surprise. "You've got blood on you man, you get in a tussle?"

"I found Jenna, She's… She's been raped and beaten by members of the Sons of Abaddon." His voice lowered to a whisper

"What…?" Tank glared at him, his face contorting in rage. "Where are the fuckers?"

"Dead, but we have to get Jenna out of here." He glanced back up at the mirrored window.

"All right, I'll get my truck, take the emergency exit in the VIP section, the fire exit up there hasn't got an alarm system on it. Tiff's taken me out there a couple of times for a 'private dance' or two." He glanced around to make sure they weren't spotted by Dimitri or Vladimir.

Firebird gripped his arm in thanks and headed back up the stairs to Jenna. The bed was empty, the covers gone.

"Jenna?" Firebird called. He heard a soft sob coming from a darkened corner of the room, her foot stuck out in the dim shaft of light, painted toenails exposed. She slowly pulled her foot from the light, trying to huddle into as small a space as she could.

"Baby, it's me. Firebird." He moved slowly, crouching down to kneel beside her. "I'm going to get you out of here baby." He spoke with tenderness as he reached out toward her. She pulled away, sobbing harder, her coverlet-covered body shaking hard in the shadows.

"It's all right, baby." He soothed as he put his arms around her, holding her close to him. He carefully lifted her into his arms and held her tight against his chest. He stood, opened the door and hurried out. The door to the fire escape beckoned and he hurried into the crisp night.

The truck below the stairs was idling, the low rumble quieter than a Harley. He hurried down the stairs with his precious cargo. Tank jumped out of the driver's side and opened the passenger side for him. Once Firebird and Jenna were safely in the cab, he shut the door and jumped into the driver's seat.

"Where to?" he asked as he put the truck in gear and began to move out of the parking lot.

"Mom's place."

"You sure about that? If your pop is there…"

"If he's there, I'll deal with it." Firebird snapped. He was fuming Jenna had been hurt again. "Right now I think she needs a woman's help, and my Mom is the only one I trust right now with her."

"Okay, brother." Tank shifted the truck into gear and pulled out of the back parking lot of the strip club.

Jenna closed her eyes and trembled in Firebird's arms.

Chapter Nineteen

She was swathed in warm, soft sheets but her body cried out in agony. Between her legs hurt so badly, she was afraid to get up and use the bathroom which she so desperately needed.

Her left eye was swollen shut and she could barely move her jaw. Her body was stiff and she could taste the rawness in her mouth from the torn tissue where her teeth had ripped the inside of her mouth when the men had hit her.

The room she woke up in was strange, but it had a familiar scent to it. Pictures of Harleys and half-nude chicks draped over classic American muscle cars and old style Harleys adorned the walls. She ran a hand over the swelling of her cheeks, wincing at the pain and the damage her fingers encountered.

Her wrists had been bandaged and the smell of antiseptic cream arose from the warmth of her pores. She groaned softly as she sat up, working the damaged muscles of her battered body in ways she knew weren't ready to be moved. She was clothed in an old Harley Davidson tee shirt, and a pair of shorts with the drawstring pulled snug around her waist to keep them in place.

Muffled voices rose from behind the closed door. She slowly swung her feet over the side of the bed, gasping in pain. Her legs barely held her up as she made her way around the wall to the door. She cracked the door open slightly and peered out. Her eyes watering at the bright light of the hallway when it hit her sensitive eyes.

"…I don't care who this whore is, you are going to return her to Rodchenko. The Club has voted son, we can't risk losing the Russian connections." A stranger's voice sounded loud and angry down the hall. She crept closer toward the light.

"Fuck Dad, did you even see her? How bad they beat her? It wasn't Rodchenko, it was the Sons of Abaddon. Rodchenko let them do this to her." Firebird's voice. "What if it were Mom?"

"It wasn't your Mom they did this to, son, it was Rodchenko's girl, he allowed it."

"I was never Rodchenko's girl." Jenna's voice breached her lips, weak but vehement as she leaned against the corner of the wall, clutching the corner for support.

"Jenna." Firebird jumped to his feet and helped her over to the kitchen table where an older, more grizzled version of him sat.

She winced as she settled down on the cushioned seat.

"And, you might want to rethink your association with them… the Sons of Abaddon bragged to Rodchenko and made plans with him while they… they…" She coughed, trying to force the words out. "…raped me." She whispered. Her body shook as the painful memories took over her body and hot tears began to fall. Firebird placed his hand on her shoulder before he left to make her a cup of tea.

His father watched her, trying to figure out if she was lying or not. "Why would that concern me?" He leaned back in his chair and crossed his arms over his broad chest.

"Because they are going to take over your business, kill your members and steal the shipments that Rodchenko has going with you. They said something about guns, and drugs. I don't care what it is, I care about Firebird, and I don't want to see him hurt." She placed her beaten hands on the table as Firebird settled a warm cup of tea in front of her. She reached for it, but her trembling hands didn't want to co-operate, hot liquid spilling over the cup to soak into the bandages. Firebird sat down next to her and helped her to sip the tea.

"You care about my son that much, eh?" Dozer eyed her over.

She nodded. "I do." Firebird lifted the cup to her lips, she put her hands under the cup to support it and guide how much he would give her. She swallowed the tea, it was sweet and warming, helping her to feel better.

"All right, I need you to tell me everything that they said." He sighed. "But I'll need to have some of my men hear too, so we'll take you around to the clubhouse.

"Are you sure that's a good idea, dad? She's not really in any condition to travel."

"I'll call church in the morning, we're not scheduled for any shipments with Rodchenko for a couple of days." He turned his gaze back to Jenna. "And you, my girl, need to recall every little detail they said in your presence. Until then, get some rest. I'm sure my son will look after you." He got up, pushing the chair out behind him.

"I'll have some of the brothers on watch here, in case anyone decides to come pay us a visit. I'll be back at the clubhouse. Got a potential shit storm brewing with Rodchenko, especially with you and Tank taking off with his girl before he was finished with her. Can't believe the bastard had it on camera." Dozer stood and sauntered out of the room.

Firebird followed his father, leaving Jenna sitting at the table.

She heard their voices speaking low before the front door closed and the rumble of a Harley starting up resounded through the house.

Firebird came back into the kitchen. He looked at her for a few minutes before he sat down beside her again. "How are you feeling?"

"Sore, tired, exhausted." *Lost.* She sighed. He pulled her gently into his arms, kissing the top of her head.

"I'm sorry I wasn't there for you before. I'm sorry I didn't come back when you were in the hospital." He whispered against her hair. She broke, weeping as she reached up to him, her hands reaching around his middle to hold him tight.

"Jenna, I can't be without you, I love you, baby." He felt her sob harder against his chest. His hand stroked her hair, caressing and soothing her.

"I'm so tired." She spoke softly, wanting to tell him how she felt, but unable to form the words in her broken state. She felt as though she was beyond love. After all, why would Firebird want such a broken doll as she?

"Come on." Firebird stood and gathered her into his arms. Lifting her easily, he carried her back into his bedroom and settled her into the bed. He dragged his boots and jeans off before he slid into bed with her, pulling the covers up over her. She watched him with wide, dark eyes.

"Jenna, I meant what I said." He lay on his side, reaching out to gently caress her cheek. "I love you."

A single tear broke free, rolling down her face. Firebird leaned over and kissed her with tenderness. She rolled over, laying against his body, snuggling in for the warmth, peace and protection he offered her.

"Thank-you," she whispered. "For being with me."

Firebird pulled her close, his arms secure around her battered body. He would take his time with her, let her heal before he asked to make love to her. Within minutes, her breathing had calmed and she was fast asleep.

Firebird held her for hours before he too drifted off.

Chapter Twenty

The smell of bacon and eggs cooking roused him, along with the soft humming of his mother. He had been grateful she had still been awake when they'd brought Jenna in the previous night. She had taken over, ordering Firebird about while he settled an unconscious Jenna on his mother's couch. He had helped her to bathe Jenna's wounds and bind them with bandages and plasters.

His mother worked at a clinic, as a medical receptionist and knew her way around a first aid kit. It was handy knowledge, especially for a biker's Old Lady.

"How is the girl?" she asked when she felt him put his arms around her and hugged her tight. He might have been a tough son-of-a-bitch but he still had a soft spot for his mother.

"She's okay, I think." He leaned against the edge of the counter, then pushed himself up to sit on the countertop. He watched as his mother put bacon and eggs on a plate with toast onto a plate for him and handed him a cup of coffee.

"Get your ass off the counter!" She snapped, swatting his leg with the greasy spatula.

"Ouch!" he griped.

"I can still swat you like the best of them, sonny boy," his mother chided him.

He slipped off the counter, grabbed breakfast from his Mom and took the plate to the table.

"I'm making her some oatmeal; it will probably be best if she's got bruising in and around her mouth." His mother turned back to the stove.

"Mom, can I borrow your car today? I have to take Jenna to the club. Dad wants her to sit in, she has some information."

"I need the car for work, but how about I drop you both off there?"

"That would be great, thanks Mom. I left in a hurry last night and my bike is still at the club."

His mother nodded as she stirred the pot of oatmeal. "All right, eat your breakfast then go and get ready. Wake your girl up, and I'll get ready for work, We'll leave after she's eaten."

Firebird downed his bacon and eggs before he removed his plate to the sink, stealing a spoonful of the warm oatmeal from the pot. His mother smacked him on the hand. "Go get your girl up, she needs to get back to a normal routine as soon as possible. It's important you give her time to heal but don't allow her to wallow."

"Yeah, yeah, I'm going." Firebird kissed his mother on the cheek.

He padded down the hall to his door, pushing it open to find the bed empty and Jenna curled up in a tight ball in the corner of the room, rocking slowly on the balls of her feet. Her head tucked in her arms, folded across her knees.

"Jenna?" He approached her slowly. "Baby, are you all right?" She reacted with a sob and drew back at his touch. "Baby, it's Firebird." She looked up at him, her eyes red rimmed and tortured.

"You left me," she accused. Her agonised expression broke his heart. "I woke up and you were gone. I was terrified and didn't know what to do. I'm afraid they'll come back for me." Tears cascaded down her swollen and bruised face.

"I wasn't far; I'll never be far from you again. I promise." He eased her into his arms and sat holding her secure in the circle of his arms while she lay her head against his chest. His mother knocked on the door and looked in.

"Brett, sweetheart, we need to get going soon."

Firebird nodded. "I know Mom. Won't be long, just give us a few more minutes, okay?"

"All right honey, I've got clothes in the bathroom for your girl."

"Thanks, Mom." He held her close when his mother left them, pulling the door closed behind her.

He helped Jenna to her feet after a few minutes, coaxing her up. He kept his arms around her as they made their way to the bathroom. Jenna undressed, her movements slow, her pain obvious in the paling of her face and the burning tears threatening to spill down her face again.

"I need to use the bathroom." She spoke so softly Firebird almost missed it.

"Of course." He left the bathroom "I'll be right outside, baby." He pulled the door closed and waited for her to finish. He heard the flushing of the toilet and knocked on the door. Nothing. He knocked again before he opened it to find her looking at herself in the mirror. Her beautiful face a landscape of bruises and dark red scabs where the skin had been broken and the healing process had begun. A look of pure hatred and desolation marred her face. Deep down he knew it was all aimed at herself, and she was going downhill, fast.

Jenna's demeanor changed, her body tensed. With a scream that rivalled a Banshee's wail, she pulled her hand back into a fist and smashed it through the mirror. Broken glass crashed into the sink and onto the floor. Shards large and small glittered in the bathroom light as they fell, tinkling to the tiles below.

He saw her legs crumple beneath her as her hands reached for her face, hiding it from the world as heavy sobs wracked her body. He burst through the bathroom door to catch her before she hit the floor. The bastards had broken her spirit as well as her body.

Her body would heal before her spirit, but Firebird was determined to be by her side, every step of the way. He cradled her, rocking her gently like she was a child to be soothed after a horrendous nightmare.

"Mom!"

She rushed to the bathroom to find her son holding the young woman as she sobbed brokenly. She had heard the smash of the vanity mirror and observed the destruction of both mirror and girl. Broken glass crunched beneath her shoes as she came to sit beside the young woman, cradled in her son's arms.

"Shh, it's all right, honey, you're safe now." His mother stroked Jenna's head as Firebird rocked her in his arms. "They're not going to hurt you again."

"I can clean this up Mom, you're going to be late for work. Can you call Dad and see if Tank can come pick us up?"

"No," She turned the taps on in the bath, putting the plug in the drain. "I'll call in sick to work; Lord knows I have some sick days up my sleeve. She needs care, son." His mother looked at Jenna. "She's going to need a lot of love and understanding to get through this." "I'll call your dad and tell him, the boys can come here. She's in no condition to travel."

"You sure you're okay with that Mom?" Firebird asked. His mother never allowed the brothers to conduct club business at the house. Sure, they'd had barbecues and parties, but they were all social events. This meeting would be different.

"Yes, I'm sure." She sighed. "I'll call him, just get her into the bath and let her relax, clean up the glass and we'll redress her wounds. Call me if you need me." She left Firebird and Jenna in the bathroom.

He carefully undressed her, pulling his oversized shirt off her small body. He grimaced in empathy at the bruises that marred her perfect breasts, the bite marks that still looked raw over the areolas and nipples. The shallow, but ragged cuts in her side had been caused by a sharp knife, and the open wounds where they had whipped her back oozed with blood. He felt sick to his stomach at her condition, and he was glad the bastards had paid with their own lives, but it wasn't enough. He wanted to make Rodchenko and his bastard nephews pay too.

He poured antiseptic solution into the warm bath before he shut the water off and helped Jenna into the water. She hissed at the sting of the antiseptic as it penetrated her open wounds. Firebird knelt beside her, gently running a washcloth over her body. Jenna held her knees up under her chin, her arms wrapped around them and a vacant look in her once vibrant eyes.

"You're so beautiful, my Jenna." He whispered as he bathed her wounds and tried to wipe clean her spirit of the bad memories she had earned at the hands of the men who had held her for their pleasure. "I promise, sweetheart, I won't let them hurt you again."

She lowered her head, hiding her battered face behind the rise of her knees and allowed the tears to fall

His mother knocked on the door. "Your father and the men will be here in a half hour, we need to get her ready." She entered with some fluffy towels in her hands. "Come on sweetheart, let's get you out and dry." She coaxed Jenna from the bath. Firebird helped her up, before he retreated to the closed seat of the toilet while his mother took over.

Jenna stepped into the warm towel Firebird's mother held open for her. She felt safe in the warm fluffiness that wrapped around her like a toddler's security blanket. The kindly woman patted the towel softly over her body, drying her off while Firebird watched. His face a range of emotions from anger at the damage the bastards had caused her, to sorrow, and hope, that she might come back to him.

The faint rumble of a group of motorcycles rose in a muffled crescendo through the house. Jenna tensed in the embrace of the towel.

"I think that's your father and the boys, go and see. I'll help Jenna dress."

Firebird nodded and headed downstairs.

He took hold of his piece, nestled in the waistband of his jeans, the grip a comfort in his hand, lest the roar of the bikes outside herald the arrival of the Sons of Abaddon. Relief surged through him when he opened the door a crack to see his father and the brothers out front of his parent's house. He opened the door to let them all in.

"Where is she?" his father asked.

"She had a bad turn, Mom's taking care of her upstairs."

"Will she be able to speak to us?" Dagger asked.

"I hope so, but be gentle with her. She's not in a good way. She's been badly beaten and abused by those bastards."

"Yeah nice job on them by the way. We're up four to one with those assholes taken out. Abaddon took out one of our boys on the way to visit his girlfriend last night." His father shook his head, his face grim.

"Who?" Firebird felt sick. The men gathered before him, and those who were still at the club, were his family. Men who had helped raise him when his father took him and his mother to the clubhouse. Men who had come to this very house for barbeques and Fourth of July celebrations, but never, ever club business.

"Little Mick." A sombre silence fell over the group when Dagger spoke.

Firebird remained silent for a moment before speaking out of respect for his fallen brother. "Shit. I guess we knew this was coming. Abaddon brothers have been at our throats even before I torched the car."

His father clapped a hand on his son's shoulder. "Very true, and if what your little girl in there has to say is true, then the Russians might have provided them with a way to fuck us over good."

"Let's discuss this inside." Ollie nodded toward the open door.

Two prospects remained outside, keeping an eye on the bikes and watching for anything that might herald trouble. Firebird nodded to the two young men before he followed the group of brothers into his childhood home.

Chapter Twenty-One

It was a strange sight, a group of leather-clad bikers sitting at his mother's kitchen table. Big burly men sat awkwardly in small chairs that were snagged from any room that had one to spare. One seat was left vacant for Jenna.

His mother led her in, eased her into the chair and hovered nearby. She was worried the young girl could have another spell where she fell into the deep abyss of her terrible, crippling memories.

"Jenna." Dozer leaned forward. "Tell us everything the Abaddon boys said while you were with them."

Jenna nodded. She took a deep shuddering breath and clasped her trembling hands before her on the smooth wood of the table.

"Rodchenko… he made some kind of deal with the other club, the Sons of Abaddon I think you called them? He let them…" She paused, her throat working as she fought to stop the tears from cascading down her cheeks. "Rape me, while they filmed it. He said it was a special tape for Firebird, they said they were going to give it to him after they killed a heap of Maelstrom boys, to add to his injuries. They said they were going to hit the next few shipments, then take out the clubhouse while you were all on lock-up... or something... No, that's not right, not lock-up, lock-in…?"

"Lockdown." Dozer nodded. "That makes sense. If they had a big enough group, the bastards could get us while on lockdown, especially if they take out several shipments to thin out our numbers."

"I was in and out of it a lot, but they spoke a bit about other deals, other clubs they wanted to hit."

Firebird gently placed his hands on her shoulders, his thumbs rubbing the dip where her collarbone met the rounded muscle of her shoulder. She took a shuddering breath. "I don't remember any names, not theirs or other clubs, but they said *other clubs* like they want to take over the area or something." She ran her fingers over a grain of wood inlaid on the tabletop, absentmindedly tracing the grains pattern with a trembling fingertip.

Dozer harumphed. "I think we have enough for now. Go back and rest. Thank you, honey."

Jenna stood, her body shook.

"Anna, can you take her back to Firebird's room. Stay with her, darlin' and let her get some more sleep, she looks like she needs it. I'll have two prospects here working guard duty." Dozer patted his wife's arm as she helped Jenna back down the hallway to the bedroom.

Firebird sat down in her place; a heavy silence fell over the room.

Dozer glanced at the men surrounding him. "It looks like we might need to set up a few counter ambushes in response to the possibility that the Abaddon boys will attack our next shipments. Tommy, grab the map out of my saddlebag, would you?"

Tommy got to his feet and hurried out to Dozer's bike. He returned moments later and handed the maps to his president. Dozer spread them out on the table, his finger tracing the fine inked lines marking the roads.

"Here, and here, these are the best places they can ambush us, two back roads leading away from the main road. Plenty of woodland for them to use as cover and the road thins to one lane just before the bridge, perfect bottleneck to ambush. I don't want them to think we know anything. So, we play it normal, and we'll have a little surprise waiting for them when they do attack."

"No Lockdown? Firebird asked his father,

"No lockdown, business as usual. Be extra sharp-eyed for things that don't look right."

Firebird and the rest of the men nodded.

***

The rumble of the lead bikes echoed into the night on the quiet stretch of road and broke the peace of the surrounding woodland. Two bikes led the way, a truck followed with two more bikes following.

A tree laying across the road, blocking the way brought the bikes and truck to stop.

The loud *pop-pop-pop* of gunfire zinged from the woods. Bikers' bodies jerked, riddled with bullets from hidden assailants. The driver of the truck watched in horror as the bikers fell to the ground, still.

Balaclava masked men erupted from the woods, guns trained on the driver. They pulled him from the cab and tossed him to the ground. He wasn't wearing a cut, nor did he have any ink. He was a civilian trucker, hired to drive a load. He let the masked men take the truck, laying himself on the ground at the insistence of a gunman.

A new driver jumped into the cab and the truck's reversing signal sounded deafening in the eerie quiet of the night. The driver backed up and took a dirt road nearby. A black van followed, stopping to collect the gunmen who leapt into the back compartment.

The lights of the truck and van lit up the treed area before fading in the distance. The driver rose carefully and checked on the fallen bikers. They stood and pulled the bullet-proof vests from their bodies.

"Thank fuck they didn't aim for our heads." Ollie huffed, rubbing at the red marks on his body.

Tank sat up and shook his head, dirt and leaves scattering from his long curly locks. "Fuck, they popped my tire." He poked at the flat tire on the front of his bike.

"You just don't have the best luck with tires, do you, man?" Cutter, one of the rear guards slapped Tank's back. "Push it into the bushes, we'll pick it up later, I'll head back toward town and get someone to pick you both up." He moved to his bike and checked it over for damage. Finding none, he fired up the engine and tore back toward town.

Tank and Theo, the other rear guard, pushed Tank's bike into the bushes and pulled the fallen tree out of the way, off the road.

"I hope Firebird's having more luck than we are right now." He grunted as they hid his bike in the thick bushes.

***

Firebird nervously checked his piece for the umpteenth time. Dagger placed a hand on the young man's arm. Firebird looked up at him. Dagger nodded with a grim smile. "We'll get some revenge tonight, for Little Mick and your girl."

Firebird nodded. "Yeah, I don't think this is over yet, not by a long shot."

"It won't be until Rodchenko is dead and the Sons of Abaddon are gone." Dagger spoke quietly. The Maelstrom brothers nodded their agreement.

The truck rattled over the road. The men sat on shipping crates as they accompanied the Maelstrom shipment. When the truck was opened by the Sons of Abaddon, they would be getting an unwanted surprise.

The men settled in for a wait of indeterminable time as the truck continued along the rough road.

Chapter Twenty-Two

The truck came to a stop. Voices shouted back and forth and the sound of a gate opening was heard behind the heavy duty vinyl truck curtain.

Dagger raised a hand in the dim light at the back of the truck and the men moved slowly and quietly into position behind the crates. Firebird looked to Dagger, his finger itching on the trigger of his gun.

The truck jerked forward as it entered the compound. The rattle of a garage door resounded as the truck slowed.

In the dimming light, Dagger put his index finger to his lips in a command for silence as the truck stopped and the engine was killed. Voices sounded through the darkness.

"All right boys, let's see what the Maelstrom assholes brought us."

"Rodchenko had better be right about this one." Another voice said.

Firebird scowled. The voice was familiar.

"Damn pity about our boys at the strip club. I can't wait to take out those motherfuckers. We might find that sweet piece of ass Rodchenko said we could have when we hit their clubhouse."

"Keep your mind on the job, Slash," the first voice commanded. Muttered voices echoed through the warehouse as the edges of the truck curtain were released. Bright light entered the truck as the curtain was ripped to the side, revealing the crates.

"Okay boys, unload this…"

The rest of his sentence died on his lips. The crack of gunshots rang loud as Dagger, Firebird and several other members of Maelstrom rose from their hidden places and opened fire.

The Sons of Abaddon raced for cover, three fell in the hail of bullets, taken by surprise by the ambush. Firebird felt the power of each shot when he fired his gun, the bright flash blinding for a microsecond as the kickback jarred his arms and shoulders despite his relaxed stance.

Panicked shouts sounded through the warehouse as Dagger and the Maelstrom men jumped from the truck. The Sons of Abaddon, who had survived the first wave, recovered to return fire. Firebird and Dagger huddled behind a crate on the floor taking cover from the hail of gunfire.

"Fucking hell, is it always like this with you, Dagger?" Firebird asked.

"Always, 'bird." Dagger grinned as he slammed a new clip into his gun and turned to fire. The shots were rewarded with a pained grunt and the sound of a body hitting the floor as his men advanced.

Minutes later, the sound of struggles and gunshots, quietened. Dagger cast an eye around the open warehouse. "Search the place, get the truck out and we'll burn this fucking place to the ground."

The men scrambled, searching behind crates and small offices for anyone who may have been missed. A couple of gunshots stopped Dagger and Firebird in their tracks. They raced up a set of metal stairs where the sound of the gunshots had come from. Coot, one of their older members, lay on the ground at the top of the landing. Eyes wide open and a bullet wound between his eyes.

"Fuck." Firebird knelt over his fallen brother.

Dagger pushed him back against the wall as another shot was fired, the bullet pinging against the metal railing of the stairs.

"You won't take me alive, motherfuckers!" the man shouting had a distinctive Russian accent.

Dimitri Firebird thought. *Motherfucker.*

"Give it up, Dimitri." Firebird shouted back, "You've fucked us over, there's only one way this can go." He ducked back as a bullet zinged past, just missing his head.

"You know that little slut of yours, Jenna?" Dmitri called back. "She's got such a sweet pussy, Firebird. I bet you haven't had her as many times as we have. Each and every time on camera. We've sold hundreds of tapes." He laughed. The sound of a video tape being loaded into a VCR echoed through the small office. "This one here, is my personal favourite. The president of the Sons of Abaddon took her first, then the VP, then his officers. She loved it."

A video began playing, cries and moans emanated from the speakers in the office and the flashing light of a television lit up the frosted windows. Jenna's sobs of despair burned hard in Firebird's ears, his eyes clouded with the red haze of his building rage.

"You should watch this. I'm getting fucking hard just watching it." Dimitri laughed maniacally.

Firebird snarled, his gun in hand. He pulled free of Dagger's grip and ran into an adjoining office, firing at the figure huddled against the back wall. Dimitri raised his gun but was too slow; the bullet wound in his shoulder from Coot's final shot making him sluggish.

Firebird's first shot hit Dimitri in the other shoulder, the gun dropped from his hand and he tittered insanely.

"You fucker." Firebird seethed, stepping up and pushing the barrel of his gun against Dimitri's sweaty forehead. Dimitri spat at him, the glob of spittle rolling down the leather of Firebird's cut.

"Firebird." Dagger warned from behind.

"She's so sweet, so innocent, that was the biggest selling point in her films." Dimitri grimaced with the pain of his wounds.

Firebird snarled and squeezed the trigger, unloading the clip into the Russian asshole. Dimitri's body bucked, slamming against the wall, his chest and face a mess of bloodied and torn flesh.

"Fuck. Firebird, we needed him alive. He could have given us information." Dagger stood behind and observed Firebird's furiously shaking body.

"Fucker didn't deserve to live." Firebird lifted the gun to the television screen and fired two shots into the screen, killing the image and causing the set to spark.

"Let's get the fuck out of here," Firebird muttered. The smell of gasoline filtered up as the other men doused the place.

Dagger hefted Coot's body over his shoulder and carried him down the steps to the truck where he was laid amongst others of their crew who had taken less lethal injuries. Dagger got into the driver's seat and lit a cigarette. He started the truck, while Firebird took the passenger seat and the others got in the back.

"Sorry Dagger. I lost my cool back there, man." Firebird retrieved a cigarette from his pack and the flip lighter Jenna had given him. The flame flickered, illuminating his face in the dim light of the cab as Dagger backed the truck out of the warehouse. The dead bodies of the Sons of Abaddon members soaked in gasoline.

"Shit happens, kid. You'll learn, I just don't know what your Pop will do now. We could have used that asshole for information or leverage." Dagger turned the truck, aligning Firebird's side with the open door. A puddle of gasoline led up to the main pool which their brothers had poured through the warehouse and over the crates.

"You wanna do the honours?" Dagger asked, handing Firebird his lit cigarette.

"Happy to." Firebird flicked the burning smoke into the fuel. They watched for a moment as the flame blossomed and spread over the fuel, flaring up in a rising inferno. Dagger pulled the truck away and Firebird watched in the rear-view mirror as the warehouse exploded in flames.

"You've definitely got a way with fire, boy. It's fucking beautiful" Dagger reached over and ruffled the hair on Firebird's head as they drove away.

Chapter Twenty-Three

Jenna sat on the cold tiles of the shower, her skin red raw and bleeding from scrubbing at it frantically with the washcloth and her nails. Hot tears mixed with the soap and blood as it swirled down the drain.

She wanted to scrub away the filth that had buried its way under her skin from those bastards who had used her body and broken her mind. She wanted to be clean again, free, make a fresh start. But she didn't want to do it without Firebird.

She ignored the soft knocking on the bathroom door, and continued to scrub at her legs and torso. Fresh blood welled up over the self-inflicted scrapes and scratches. The cooling water ignored.

"Jenna, I'm coming in sweetheart." Anna turned the doorknob of the door to the bathroom. She pulled the curtain aside and looked down on the battered young woman. "Oh, sweetheart." She turned the water off and reached for a towel.

"Don't scratch at it, honey." She gently took Jenna's clawed fingers from the skin on her legs, watching as the raised welts oozed blood. Anna picked up the soaked washcloth and wiped the blood from the scratches as Jenna whispered over and over.

"It won't come off, it won't come off." Her fingers tore at her skin.

Anna tossed the washcloth aside and pulled Jenna into her arms, cradling the distraught girl in her arms.

"I know baby, I know." She kissed Jenna's temple. "It's not your fault sweetheart. *It's not your fault.*"

Jenna sobbed, trying to absorb the words this caring woman was telling her. She clutched at Anna, her wet body flush against the cotton shirt of Firebird's mother.

Anna wrapped the towel around Jenna and held her close while she sobbed. Finally, she was spent and became limp in her arms.

"Are you hungry, sweetheart?"

Jenna nodded, bringing a smile to Anna's face. "All right, let's get you dressed and something to eat." She helped Jenna to dress in a dress that flowed to her ankles. She dried and brushed Jenna's hair before leading her to the kitchen. She sat her down at the table and served homemade soup.

The aroma of the soup tempted Jenna and she ate hungrily while Anna busied herself in the kitchen.

Jenna's spoon clattered slightly against the bowl as her hands continued to shake. She looked to Anna. "I'm sorry."

"For what?" Anna set aside the dishes she was drying.

"For… for disturbing you. For making you miss work. For being a burden. For everything."

"Jenna." Anna sat beside her and placed a comforting arm around her. "You don't have to apologise for anything. Brett – Firebird loves you, and I can see why. Underneath the broken woman sitting before me is a strong woman, who can take the shit this life has dished out. We just need to find her and put her back together again." Anna brushed back the strands of hair that had fallen across Jenna's face. Much of her swelling had subsided since Firebird had brought her in.

"When do you think they'll be back?" Jenna asked softly.

"I don't know sweetheart; however long it takes for them to finish their club business." Anna reached for her cup of coffee on the table.

"How have you survived this life for so long?"

"With love, patience and a lot of understanding. Sometimes you can't ask the questions you want to and expect an answer."

Jenna sighed, her hand playing with the spoon in her empty bowl. "How do I get through this?" Her voice broke. "My parents moved back to Australia two months ago. I can't tell them what happened, can't put them through all this. I have no-one here. No-one I can turn to. No-one I can trust."

"Wrong." Anna wrapped her arms around Jenna. "You have us, sweetheart. Brett loves you and I think you love him too." Anna pulled back to look into the eyes of the young woman who had captured her son's heart. "You can turn to us. You can trust us."

Jenna was quiet for a moment. "I do love him, I really do. He's always been good to me. Kind, courteous, willing to help me, even if it put him in danger."

Anna smiled, taking the empty bowl and bringing Jenna a cup of tea. "Why don't you go and sit in the chair by the window, you'll probably hear them before you see them, those Harley's have quite a growl to them."

Jenna pushed herself up stiffly and moved with a slow, limping gait to the chair, where the sun shone warmly through the lace curtains. She had a good view of the street and watched the two prospects as they sat on their bikes, watching over the residence.

You're safe here… she thought to herself. *Rodchenko can't get to you.* She clutched her cup, her hands shaking so badly she had to take a large mouthful of her tea, lest it spill over her hands. The sweet brew helped to calm her, and she sat, watching the street from her window for the rest of the afternoon, waiting for her knight in shining leather to come home to her. As the day wore on, and dusk started to approach, she dozed off.

She woke to the rumbling growl of a group of Harleys coming down the street.

He's home… she thought with a smile, her body relaxing with relief for the first time in ages.

Until she heard the first shot and saw the first prospect fall.

Chapter Twenty-Four

"Something came for you while you were out." Frankie handed Firebird a large yellow envelope.

Dagger stepped up beside him. "What is it?"

Firebird felt over the envelope. The contents were thick and suspiciously shaped like video tapes.

"I've got a bad feeling about this, Pop." Firebird's gut churned.

"My office." His father nodded to the stairs which led to his office.

Firebird followed his father. Coot's body had been taken to the morgue, where one of the attendants was on their payroll and would take care of their brother's body. The other brothers, who had suffered minor injuries were being patched up by one of the town's doctors, also on the payroll.

Dozer opened the office with his key and let Firebird in. His son was agitated, and he had a feeling it had to do with whatever was on those tapes.

He turned on the TV and set the channel to VCR before reaching out and waiting for Firebird to hand him the envelope with the tapes. His son did so, grudgingly. The first tape was loaded, and the screen came to life.

The TV's speakers buzzed for a moment with the poor quality sound recording, obviously an amateur video.

Firebird and Dozer watched in horror as a woman was held down and violated by several men, all wearing Abaddon cuts. Firebird stared at the panicked face of the woman just before one of the men pulled his knife and slit her throat. His hands fisted in her auburn hair. The sick bastard licked the side of her face as her blood drained from the open cut in her neck. Her struggle was futile, her body succumbed to the blood loss and she died. The men returned to using her body before the last man groaned his climax and pulled away from the bloodied and still body.

"Fuck me." Dozer's face was ashen and his guts roiled as he just realised they'd watched a snuff film. The camera shut off for a moment before it returned. Sitting where the woman had been slaughtered like an animal, on the very bed he had laid Jenna down on when he had rescued her, sat Johnny, the Vice President of the Sons of Abaddon

"Hey Firebird, you fucking asshole piece of shit. Your whore will be the next star of the biggest selling snuff film we've ever produced. And, you'll get a front row seat to watch. Right now, our boys are taking her, and your bitch mother to the club. Good luck getting to them before Rodchenko and our boys have played with them both. I'll leave you now, with one of my personal favourites in the *Firebird's bitch* collection. Enjoy motherfucker." The camera shut off, the picture coming back in to show Jenna tied to the bed, a strange woman's head between her legs and the fat Russian fuck, Rodchenko pounding into the woman from behind.

"Mother*fucker!*" Firebird screamed.

Dozer immediately reached for the phone on his desk and dialled his home number. It rang out. He tried again and shook his head. He hung up, turned to his safe and pulled out extra ammo for his guns. He made it a habit to be armed in the clubhouse. He wanted to make sure that each and every fucker in that strip club who had something to do with this, was good and dead.

He looked to his son. "Get your head in the game, boy, if we're going to do anything to save our women, we need to get it together, now." He turned off the VCR, taking the tape from the player.

Firebird followed his father back downstairs and waited by his side as he spoke. "Everyone, get your shit together, Anna and Firebird's girl have been taken by Abaddon. We have to get them back before anything happens to them."

His men rushed to grab their weapons, some slipped bulletproof vests over their torsos, sliding their cuts back on easily over the protective apparel.

Firebird was the first on his bike, starting it up and revving it until the sounds of the engine reverberated heavily against the concrete buildings in the compound. The noise grew twentyfold as more men joined them. Tank rolled up in a truck beside him; his bike was still waiting to have its tire fixed

"Let's go get your girl and your ma." Tank shouted over the deafening roar of the engines.

Dozer started his bike and burned rubber getting out of the compound, followed by his club.

His bike ate up the miles as Firebird raced to save Jenna. His heart pounded in his chest. *I promised you I'd never let them hurt you again, Jenna. Oh baby, I'm so sorry.* He pushed down the guilt, using the pain of it to fuel the fire of anger in his belly. With his clips replenished after disposing of Dimitri back at the warehouse, he was ready to take down as many of those Abaddon pricks as he possibly could. But, there was a special bullet saved just for Johnny. Another for Rodchenko he would save for Jenna to pull the trigger, if she so chose, otherwise, he'd have no problems with doing the job himself.

Their bikes ate up the distance to the strip club, Dozer signalling for them to stop a few blocks away so they could plan their attack. A quick discussion took place.

"All right, let's get this done." Dozer cracked his knuckles menacingly.

Chapter Twenty-Five

Jenna trembled, the rough darkness of a hood over her head blinding her. She could smell the sex in the room. The blood, the fear, the tang of the metal, the acrid flavour of dust as it burned lightly on the hot lightbulbs glaring down on her. Her flesh heated, beads of sweat dribbled over her body burning her raw skin and still-open wounds. She choked out a sob when the black hood was pulled from her head. Her hands and feet were left bound.

"Ahh. My flower. My pretty one has returned." Rodchenko's rough hand caressed her face, before he pulled his hand from her broken and scratched skin and slapped her with such force her teeth cut into her bottom lip and her head snapped to the side. "Fucking whore."

Jenna felt her lip go numb, saliva and blood mixed in a glistening red strand that dripped down onto her naked chest.

"All you had to do was be a good little whore, and after the Abaddon boys had their fun, we could go back to having ours." He strode around her trembling, naked body. Her hands bound behind her, her feet tied to the chair she was sitting in. "You could have been on my arm at the most extravagant parties, and writhing under me every night in supreme ecstasy, but no, you had to go and fuck around with that bastard Maelstrom pup." He sneered, lowering his face to hers so she could smell the rotting teeth inside his mouth.

Jenna wanted to gag, and puke all over his smug features and expensive, tailored clothes, but she had no desire to bring his ire down on her harder than it already would be. She lowered her gaze.

A moan caught her attention, Anna was similarly bound, and was just regaining consciousness from the nasty strike to her head by Johnny, the Sons of Abaddon VP.

"And here's the star of our next film. Our clientele will be excited to see a Prez's old lady get fucked and snuffed." Rodchenko stepped nearer to Anna. "Especially by a rival club's men."

Vladimir entered, followed by a few members of the Sons of Abaddon, including their President. Vladimir callously reached over and gripped Jenna's naked breast, pinching it hard enough for the scabs on her skin to crack open and start bleeding again. Her cry of agony spurring the sick bastard on. "Sing for me baby, just like you do when I'm buried deep inside you."

Jenna looked away.

"So, how long until those fuckers arrive?" Johnny asked.

"Any time now," Rodchenko answered.

"I'm going to head out and see how they are going with the other project." Johnny smirked, "Save the pretty bitch for me." He winked at Jenna and turned, leaving her and Anna with Rodchenko and the other Sons of Abaddon members. Rodchenko smiled, and with a clap of his hands turned to face Jenna.

"So, shall we get started?" he rubbed his hands in child-like glee. "Who first? The whore or the mother?"

***

The roar of the large group of motorcycles rumbled through the neighbourhood. The new bouncers, wearing their Sons of Abaddon cuts bristled when they saw the group of Maelstrom members storming toward the door. Firebird raised his piece and fired.

Bang!

Bang!

The thumps of the bouncer's bodies hitting the concrete barely registered against the pumping bass of the strip club's sound system. The men moved to the inside of the club swiftly, ignoring the crowd as they watched the women gyrate their naked bodies against the shiny poles for cash. Firebird led the way up to the VIP section, taking out anyone in his way, fury clouded his vision, his father not two steps behind.

Four Abaddon members waited at the top of the stairs to the VIP room where Firebird had found Jenna just two days ago. He raised his gun to fire at the men, but his father pushed him to the side and fired instead. Firebird's ears rang with the rapport of the gunfire in the small enclosed hall. The ringing in his ears drowned out all other noise as his adrenalin pushed him toward the locked door. He kicked at the door, ignoring the dead men at his feet. The door remained closed and locked.

"Out of the way, boy." Dozer shouted, aiming his piece at the lock. He fired until the lock was destroyed, then lifted his heavy boot and kicked the door open.

"About time you boys joined us for the party." Rodchenko was barely hidden behind Jenna's trembling, naked frame. Anna was also naked and restrained by the President of the Sons of Abaddon.

"Let the women go, Nipper." Dozer ordered.

Anna whimpered in the enemy's grasp.

Firebird raised his gun and took aim at Rodchenko. "Let them go, fuckers." He snarled, his hand trembling with rage.

"But we haven't finished our movie yet. Wouldn't you like to star in your own pornographic film with this beautiful creature?" Rodchenko's hand reached around to grip Jenna's breast, his tongue slid out and licked up the side of her neck.

Firebird's face clouded with rage. "Touch her again, fucker and I'll-"

"You'll what? Shoot me?" Rodchenko turned his head to smirk at Firebird. He again licked at Jenna's naked shoulder.

Jenna whimpered, but the sound was drowned out by a cracking gunshot. Blood, bone and brain splattered her pretty face as the side of Rodchenko's head erupted from Firebird's bullet. She froze, her shock evident. A second shot rang loud in the silence following immediately after the first shot.

Dozer's cry of anguish broke Jenna from her trance to see Anna's hair flick to the side as the bullet passed through her head and embedded itself in the gaudy red wall of the VIP room.

The Earth seemed to stand still as Nipper pushed the body of Firebird's mother, Dozer's wife, to the floor and moved toward her.

One step,

Two steps

Another gunshot.

A heartbeat

Two heartbeats.

His body hit the floor, his eyes open and unseeing to the world around him as the two men who still lived and breathed ran to their fallen wife and mother.

Jenna's breath was harsh in her ears as she watched Dozer and Firebird, two strong, tough bikers crumble at Anna's side. This was the woman who had loved the two men with her whole heart. A generous, caring woman who had helped her through the trauma of her ordeal.

Jenna crumpled to the floor, her arms hugged tight around her naked body as sobs wracked her uncontrollably.

Dozer held his wife in his arms, his body shaking with sobs as his brothers surrounded the loving couple.

Tank rushed in, took one look at the scene and noticed Jenna, curled on the floor. He pulled the comforter from the bed, wrapped it around Jenna and swept her into his arms. He covered carried her out, away from the blood, the loss the death.

The strip club had emptied with the commotion of gunshots and screaming.

Jenna snuggled against Tank's chest, hiding in the comforter, yet finding no comfort in her grief. Her mind blanked, finding solace in nothingness, peace in the darkness to which her mind retreated.

Chapter Twenty-Six

Dozer stood, his beautiful wife held close against him. Firebird pulled a black silk sheet from the bed and covered his mother's naked body while his father openly wept for his dead wife.

He'd been dimly aware of Tank taking Jenna out of the VIP room, away from the carnage and death. He followed his father as he carried his mother's body from the room. The men stood back quietly out of respect.

She had been Dozer's woman from age nineteen, when he was a twenty-two-year-old man. They had been together for only one week before he was deployed to Vietnam. He returned two and a half years later, and joined the Brotherhood of The Maelstrom MC, trying to find his way after the horrors of war. He found Anna working at a diner, her one-and-a-half-year-old boy in a playpen in the employee's break room. He had never thought she'd keep her promise to wait for him to come back, but his heart soared when she explained that she had.

Anna had been understanding, knowing he needed companionship from fellow returned soldiers, in a life that, sometimes, held as much danger as a war zone. She had loved him at his worst and cherished him at his best. She had waited for him when he was in prison and raised their son with love and compassion.

She had helped his chapter grow, attended club parties, helped the men when they needed a sympathetic ear or a bandage to a bullet graze.

The men all walked behind Dozer and Firebird silently, respectfully through the now deserted strip club. Lights flashing, the DJ booth empty, the record finished on the turntable, static scratching through the speakers. Motorcycle boots crunched on broken glass and kicked at dead bodies. Vladimir's dead gaze watched the silent parade lifelessly, slumped over the bar, a broken bottle of vodka in his hand. The men of Maelstrom had done their work, finishing off the Russians and the remaining Abaddon members.

The doors opened revealing the bright sunlight and the sound of sirens in the distance.

"Burn it." Dozer ordered as they departed the strip club, not looking back.

Six of the brothers turned back to the bar, grabbing what liquor they could and pouring it over every surface that would burn. One ran to the kitchen and turned the gas to full on the cooktop, letting it flow into the air. The last man in the club lit the match that would feed the fuel and bring the place of sin and death to the ground in a fiery blaze.

They ran from the club as Dozer settled his wife's body in the backseat of Tank's truck. After hollering instructions to Tank, he ran to his bike and rode out of the strip club's parking lot, leading the truck. Firebird and an honour guard of six followed behind.

***

Jenna shivered in shock. She was still wrapped in the comforter. Tank had dropped Anna's body off at the morgue, Dozer carrying her silk-wrapped body through the back entrance doors. Tank drove Jenna back to the Maelstrom MC's club, leaving Dozer and Firebird at the morgue saying farewells to their Anna.

She sat at the bar, dressed in clothes borrowed from one of the Storm Girls. Her hands twitched with raw nerves. Tank was pouring a shot of whiskey to help calm her, when the rumbling motorcycle engines of the returning men, vibrated the walls and rattled the windows.

Tank pulled out all the shot glasses from under the bar. He poured the last of the whiskey into the glasses, then opened a new bottle to fill the empty ones. The liquor spilled over the glasses and onto the bar. Tank didn't care. In a way, he too had lost a mother with the death of Anna. He glanced up as the men entered, all grim, somber. Quiet. The loss heavy on their minds and in their hearts. Tank handed out shots to each man as he came forward to claim a glass.

When all the men had their shot in hand, Tank looked each and every one in the eye before he raised his glass. "To Anna, may our beautiful lady rest in peace."

"To Anna." The club chorused in unison, tossing back the amber liquid. When the last of the liquor had been swallowed, the men raised their arms and threw their shot glasses down to shatter on the tiled floor.

Tank watched Jenna as she threw back her own shot and smashed the glass on the floor to join the others. He nodded his respect to her, a small smile gracing his lips.

***

Anna's body lay pale on the cold steel of the morgue's examination table. The matted blood and brain matter had been cleaned by Alan Rook, a former prospect who had a way with death. Though he hadn't made the cut with the MC, he still helped them with instances where a body might need to be taken care of off the books, but with an official cause of death.

Rook came in quietly and placed the death certificate in its yellow envelope on an empty table near where Anna's body lay. Officially, she had died of a brain aneurysm.

Dozer leaned over his wife's body, hot tears trickled down his reddened cheeks. Eyes red and swollen from crying. He reluctantly pulled himself from her cold, stiff body. Reaching out, he pulled his son to him.

Firebird put his head on his father's shoulder and mourned his mother. His body shook, and he stepped back from his father's embrace. He kept a hand over his mouth as he felt the rage build inside him. With a primal scream, borne of grief and rage ripping from his throat, his muscles bunched and he swept through the room. Small stainless steel containers holding cotton swabs and mortuary bottles containing liquids smashed to the floor, victims of his uncontrolled grief and anger.

He pounded his fists into stainless steel benchtops until bloody imprints were left in the newly dented surfaces. His father's arms went around him, attepting to soothe and hold his son's rage at bay. Firebird sobbed hard and turned to his father; he leaned his head against his father's shoulder and sobbed while his hands fisted his dad's cut.

"She's not hurting, son. She's at peace. She didn't suffer as the bastards intended." His father's voice sounded thick and broken as he held his grieving son. "I swear on my cut, we'll make every one of those

Abaddon bastards pay in blood. We'll wipe them off the face of the earth." His father gripped his son's shoulder.

Rook cleared his throat. Having heard the commotion, he surveyed the damage. "I'm sorry Dozer, Firebird, we need to move quickly if we're going to get her…" he paused, trying to find the right words. "To get her into the… to…"

"Cremate her, Yes… I know, Rook. I know." Dozer wiped the tears from his eyes. He leaned down and kissed Anna's pale lips tenderly and gathered her limp body in his arms. He held her tight for a few moments before he lay her back down. His final goodbye.

"Goodbye, my love. I'll see you in the next life." He kissed her one final time.

Firebird watched as his father released his mother and turned to leave. "We'll wipe them out son, every last chapter."

Firebird nodded, emotion knotting in his throat. He was left alone with his mother's body.

Firebird approached her, lifted her hand to his lips and kissed her knuckles before he pressed it to his forehead. Tears cascaded down his face. A grief so powerful it tore him apart.

"Thank-you Mom, for being there for me, for being there when I needed you the most. Thank-you for looking after Jenna. Thank-you for being my mother. For guiding me in life, even if the road I took wasn't the one you would have liked me to take. I'd gladly walk it again, in this life and the next. Because I got to know you. I got to have you as my mom." He studied her pale face, ignoring the damage to the side of her head. He leaned over and kissed her cheek before he placed her hand over her still heart.

He straightened, and wiped his eyes. Nodding to Rook, he left the morgue.

Chapter Twenty-Seven

"I can't stay here any longer, Pop," Firebird admitted to his father. It had been two months since the funeral for his mother. Jenna had been by his side constantly. They had moved slowly toward lovemaking but kept away from sex for now. Jenna still suffered mentally from the abuse she had endured. They were both healing, finding each other, rediscovering themselves.

Dozer's face was drawn. He had taken a few weeks leave to mourn. No one had heard from Johnny, the V.P. of the Sons of Abaddon. In the past week the Maelstrom brothers had hunted down and slaughtered every last member of the local Sons of Abaddon chapter. War was well and truly underway.

"I have to get Jenna out of here, there's too many bad memories." He sighed as he ran his hand over the wooden table they sat around in Church. "For both of us."

"Your Uncle's chapter in the east is struggling for numbers. Maybe you should go and see him. We can arrange a transfer. Wherever you go, take Tank, I know he'll want to be by your side. The two of you are inseparable. I'd be worried if you didn't have him by your side to keep you out of trouble." He reached over and opened his bottle of whiskey, pouring two glasses and sliding one to his son.

"Maybe he keeps me in trouble, Pop." Firebird raised an eyebrow.

"Your Mother would be proud of you son, she always was." Dozer glanced at the small urn sitting nearby. "I'll call your uncle, make the transfer, ensure the vote goes your way on his end and ours. He'll be happy to have you both there; that is if you want to go?" Dozer looked at his son.

"Yeah, that would be great. Thanks, pop."

Dozer stood to embrace his son. "As soon as you're settled, I'm going nomad."

"What?" Firebird pushed away from his father to look at him.

"Yeah, Ollie's going to take my place as president. I've served my club. It's time for me to serve myself and find who I am again."

"I understand that, Pop. I totally understand."

There was a soft knock at the door. Firebird turned to find Jenna standing there. Many of her injuries had healed, but she still had the haunted look of grief and personal trauma burning darkly behind them. Firebird stepped away from his father and took her in his arms. He kissed her softly, tenderly. She pulled away and smiled, placing her hand lovingly on his broad chest.

"Dinner's ready." She glanced from Firebird to Dozer and back again. Firebird pushed an errant strand of hair from her face.

"Thank you, baby." He kissed her cheek, gathered her hand and turned to leave.

"One moment, Jenna," Dozer called her back.

Firebird looked quizzically at his father.

Jenna's eyes widened as she looked at Firebird, uncertain. "It's okay," he whispered and kissed her cheek before releasing her hand and walking away.

Dozer studied the young woman as she stood before him. "You've got a strength about you that Anna had." He studied her for a moment. "My wife helped me through a lot of tough times. I came back from the war in Vietnam a broken man, she helped to piece me back together. I do have some days where I don't know my ups from my downs, and I have nightmares every night about my time as a soldier, but her constant strength kept me going." He sat down and ran a hand over his tired face.

"She would be proud to have called you her daughter. I wouldn't be surprised if Firebird didn't pop the question soon. He's a good man, Jenna. I too would be proud to call you daughter when the time comes."

Tears pricked Jenna's eyes.

Dozer stood and approached her slowly, placed his arms around her and embraced her. "Take care of my boy, Jenna. He needs a good woman in his life. Take care of him and he'll take care of you." He released her and she smiled.

"I love him, Dozer. He saved me from myself, even when I didn't even know I needed saving."

"He loves you very much, honey. Be happy in your life, we've seen there are no guarantees on how long we will live." He smiled at her. "Come on, dinner's probably gone cold, or those pigs downstairs have eaten it all." He took Jenna's hand and led her down to the common area where the bar had been laden with a buffet-style feast.

Firebird handed her an empty plate and stayed close while she filled their plates with food. They sat beside Dozer at the long table.

Chatter and chewing ensued, like a madhouse of starving children with few manners and language foul enough to make a nun blush. Firebird watched his brothers. Tank looked at him and he nodded, the unspoken communication between them was understood.

After the meal, Dozer headed up to the office to make the call to his brother. When he returned, he found Firebird and Jenna slow dancing, close together by the old jukebox as it played a sad old country song.

"Son, Doug said he'll expect you in a couple of weeks."

Firebird stopped dancing, holding Jenna tight against his chest.

"That's great, thanks pop."

Jenna looked up at her man. "Where?"

"California. We're going to start a new life in California, baby." Firebird held her tight. He leaned down and kissed her, feeling her melt against him.

She opened her eyes to his smile.

"It's going to be a whole new life for us, babe. A fresh start." He pulled her close for another passionate kiss.

***

In the dingy motel room, the hooker slept. The sheets twisted around her stick figure body. track lines ran up her arms and the used needle lay abandoned, but ready for another hit when she awoke.

The man sitting at the table reached over and picked up the phone on the first jangling ring. "Yeah." He listened for a few moments while the caller spoke. "Good, keep tabs on them, I have a few contacts in chapters on the east coast, I'll be there in a few months, it's best I lay low for a while."

The voice spoke again. "Yeah, Firebird will burn, but this time, he won't rise from the ashes." The man hung up and stared through the blinds at the empty car park.

The whore moaned as she stretched in the rumpled sheets. "Johnny? You coming back to bed baby?"

"Soon." He said, "Soon." Just like his revenge, it would be soon.

The End…